Drawn to the Night

Drawn to the Night

1st Edition

Story concept and text © 2025 by Dennis Kafalas

Cover design © 2025 Amidei Arte.

Editing, print preparation, formatting, back cover summary, and final cover design © 2025 Amidei Arte and © 2025 Staback Author Services.

Books may be ordered through popular, online retailers, Page Turner Books, Inc.'s online store, or by contacting the publisher at:

Page Turner Books, Inc.
222 N. Lafayette St., Suite 11
Shelby, NC 28150

Visit our website at www.ptbooksinc.com or contact us via email at contact@ptbooksinc.com. Page Turner Books, Inc.'s name and logo are copyright of Page Turner Books, Inc.

iBook ISBN: 978-1-965788-85-1
Kindle ISBN: 978-1-965788-86-8
Hardcover ISBN: 978-1-965788-87-5
Paperback ISBN: 978-1-965788-88-2

Library of Congress Control Number: 2025933824

Printed in the United States of America. First Printing: September 2025

ATTENTION CORPORATIONS AND ORGANIZATIONS:

Most Page Turner Books, Inc. books are available at quantity discounts with bulk purchase for educational, business, or sales promotional use. For information, please call or write:

Special Markets Department, Page Turner Books, Inc.
222 N. Lafayette St., Suite 11, Shelby, NC 28150
Telephone: (702) 606-1775

Drawn to the Night

Dennis Kafalas

Shelby NC USA

Dedication

For Kindra, Jeff, Vaeh, Cole, and Lilly—and to all
families blended with love.

Acknowledgements

Thanks to my wife, Barbara, and friend, Diane Lebrun,
for their editing and ideas.

"Grief changes shape, but it never ends."

~Keanu Reeves

1

She was an unusual child, at best. To others her age, she was strange. It was during her third foster home placement at the age of four when Jamella Garcia's peculiar habits developed. So many staring, curious faces in homes either dusty or dark, carpeted or creaky, overwhelmed the child. The loud German Shepard at one home was scary, and cats made her eyes water. It was easier to play with her stuffed butterfly, Lucy, and imagine a quiet world than to process all that was new.

The scatter of used toys or puzzle pieces was of no interest, but moving colors were. Jumping in puddles caused the liquid sky and clouds to wobble, while twirling and falling autumn leaves animated color. Animals and birds fascinated her to where she had to create pictures of them. Soon, all the blank paper, colored pencils, and crayons to be found were kept in her school backpack.

The girl drew no matter where, and in time created a colorful and life-like batch of sketches rolled up and placed into used paper towel sleeves. This ability separated Jamella from others, and provided a confident sense of self.

The sketches became her family, and she was always looking for more. When she arrived at the fifth, and latest—a suburban home placement—owls were a passion.

Twelve-year-old Jamella Garcia-Pel tracked the sights and sounds of the Faith Hill Middle School cafeteria with the calm of a Long-Eared Owl, the latest obsession. To the plop-plop of untied sneakers upon the tile floor, Jamella turned her head and wiggled an ear as she imagined the owl would.

"You're doing that weird thing again with your neck," her tablemate, Hannah said, who had sat with Jamella when she first arrived in grade four.

Hannah was kind, but others avoided Jamella and her awkward quirks, like Jamella's habit of eating from the lunch bag balanced on her lap because she could not watch others chew. The sight of crumbs and greasy table fingerprints turned her stomach, so she kept her eyes closed and tried not to imagine bits of chewed food splatting onto the table inches from her.

The proper untangling, too, of a plastic sandwich wrapper with the intention of returning the Saran to its smooth, unused state was now a habit. Jamella flattened each crease, her fingertip sensing the imperfection made by the fold until the happy yelp of a student, or the crash of a tray broke the spell. Oftentimes, too, the glowy flash of a necklace or earring held her attention.

"Stop it! God, Jamella," a classmate would say, "that's so weird."

Often, she ate only half of a plain ham sandwich and not the crust, which upset her mother, Laura.

"Aren't you hungry?" she asked. "Or are you too busy talking with your friends?"

Jamella would shrug, not interested in how much she ate or the cafeteria clatter and chatter, which was a maddening jumble of sights, sounds, smells, and, lately, rules about what was weird, not cool, or stupid. The sideways glances of others were obvious, as was her black-brown skin—a chocolate smudge upon a white blouse—in a world of pale faces.

The owl saw all, and she knew they thought her different, weird, and not just because she was a new kid. She was the odd ball, the freckle-faced adopted one.

So what, she thought, if her skin was different or that she wouldn't write unless a pencil had a perfect point or the sheet of paper was without a bent corner or wrinkle. What was wrong with that, she demanded of Laura.

"When did everything become such a big deal?" Jamella lamented, to which Laura wondered as well of her adopted daughter, the budding teen.

"You're not getting much classwork done," Laura said, worried her teachers were right.

Jamella, they noted, was fussy to the point of obsession. They suggested an observation by the school psychiatrist, but Laura opted to wait, hoping it was just a tic, not a symptom. But the changes in her adopted daughter's behaviors became harder to ignore. Always quiet, she was the last to speak in class or to join others at play. She had an intense, focused quiet that framed her days and nights.

Laura knew Jamella needed time to adjust to a forever home. She had moved into Laura's the winter of grade three and finished the year taxied to her former school in the city. Laura worried she might miss some friends there and at her foster home, but it was not the case. Jamella seemed detached from the home, thanking her foster parents and Mary, her caseworker, by shaking hands, but no hugs.

Jamella left holding a small, fuzzy orange and black butterfly, while wearing a plastic backpack. Laura carried a paper grocery bag not quite full of clothes.

She drove the girl, noticing how Jamella's eyes shone with interest as they passed through different neighborhoods, but the girl remained silent. She was happy to leave foster life. She had come to understand that foster parents did their best but much of what happened—the teasing, bullying, lying, and petty theft—occurred without their knowledge.

Unless an adult had witnessed the slight, insult, or punch, only then would a "cut it out" or worse, the loss of dessert or an early bedtime would be the punishment.

At home, they added the remaining clothes to a dresser, and left the backpack by the door. Jamella slipped the butterfly under a pillow on her bed.

"Do you always tuck it in that away?"

Jamella nodded.

"Lucy likes it there. It's quiet."

And safe, Laura thought.

The moment was more than Laura could process. She'd had Jamella over many times to adjust to switching foster homes, but something about a hidden stuffed animal brought too many thoughts and feelings for Laura to resolve. She would think later of this first night, and of the many things brought to mind, but it was Jamella's vulnerability Laura remembered most, from watching a nine-year-old place a favorite stuffed toy safely out of sight.

What does a child learn from moving place to place with no parent to anchor her? To make her feel safe or loved? To let her feel part of a family she is connected to, has history with, a cozy nest within to grow and eventually fly from?

Laura learned during foster parent training that children get a sense for family life in the system, but Laura wondered.

"Wouldn't it make sense," Laura asked of the trainer, "that the better the home environment—the more loving and empathetic—the harder it was to move to another?"

"Yes," Mary said. "Foster care isn't perfect, but it's the best option. And, let's not forget, children are resilient, too."

While Laura outwardly agreed, she had doubts. Resilience was unique to each child, and Jamella *had* developed ways to cope through compulsively drawing and by adopting an unassuming school profile. After all, what else could anyone who had moved from home to home do? What choice was there?

Jamella, as did the others, rode upon the waves of uncertainty like survivors in a raft, their buoyancy challenged by life's ebb and flow. Along the way, some would find themselves in over their heads, but not with Jamella. At least, gratefully, not now and not ever, Laura hoped, it was not pity that led to Jamella's adoption.

Soon after Laura agreed to foster Jamella, they developed an easy relationship.

"We're like cats, Jamella. We like being home, like the quiet, and our space," Laura had said one Sunday in May while Jamella sat with her in the den, drawing at Laura's desk.

It was then that she considered adopting the girl.

Laura spoke to Mary, whose eyes lit up with the possibility.

"She doesn't have a biological parent, and I know she'd like to be part of a family."

Laura asked to review Jamella's file so she would have a complete sense of the girl's past. It was difficult for Laura to read but furthered her resolve to adopt.

Jamella had been taken by child welfare when she was three months old. Jamella's estranged twenty-year-old father, while standing in the back hallway of a four-decker tenement house, shot her seventeen-year-old mother twice in the chest. The police arrived after the man had taken his own life, the baby asleep in a child carrier set on the kitchen table. The woman had returned from a Friday afternoon trip to the market—ice cream leaking from a plastic bag placed on the counter by the fridge—when the police found Jamella.

For a second, the image of two blood-splattered dead bodies came to Laura, but she blinked it away.

At the age of two and a half, Jamella moved to another home for toddlers and shared a bedroom with a four-year-old white girl in a house with five other children. It was here that she learned to watch her belongings, do small chores, avoid conflict, and keep to herself. When she later moved to a home in the city for the school-aged, she developed a toughness.

Jamella did not like yelling, but she was ready to fight, and she learned to handle herself with a precise aggression. At the school library, she watched self-defense videos for girls and knew the value of a well-placed kick. The ability to protect herself gave her a ninja-like confidence. Jamella avoided conflict rather than engage in it, but was confident she could handle trouble.

The girl settled into life as a foster child attending an urban school, had a casual school friend or two, but kept to herself more and more as her interest in drawing grew.

Jamella filled many school notebooks with pencil sketches until Mary bought her drawing tablets. Soon, the bedrooms at the foster home hung some of the beagle, bulldog, and pug sketches she had made. Her classmates knew her as the girl who made "awesome pictures," but at Faith Hill Elementary, she was the "weird black kid who drew all the time."

Still, she was happier with Laura, had a friend in Hannah who, like Jamella, was quietly confident. Being around all-white suburban tweens, in an all-white school and community was awkward for Jamella. She settled in, though, not needing to worry at home about something valuable being taken or keeping the precious, ruffled and threadbare butterfly with her in a school bag.

She knew right off that Laura was different, kind and considerate, and wanted Jamella to be happy, so the girl relaxed, happy to have her own space and bedroom.

Since Laura was a certified foster parent, the adoption process went smoothly. After a morning at Family Court, Jamella was legally adopted, and she spent the afternoon meeting for the first time her cousins and Laura's family, who came from out-of-town to witness the ceremony.

Later, when the day was over and Laura and Jamella readied for bed, the girl asked, "Do they like me?"

Laura stood by the wall, her hand on the overhead light switch, as the sounds of katydids' chirps slipped in under a barely open window sash.

She looked at her daughter, whose face rarely ever betrayed her true thoughts, and said, "Sure they do. It's always awkward at first. Even for me, sometimes. I don't see them as often as I should. We all get busy . . ."

Placing the latest unfinished sketch at the foot of the bed, Jamella asked, "Why do you all live in different places?"

Laura sighed.

"Followed my boyfriend here, but we broke up and I didn't go back. Business was going well and I'd made some friends, too. Honestly, going with a man somewhere far from home, well, let that be a warning to you."

"Yup. I know. Boys are stupid."

The girl rolled onto her side when Laura turned the light off.

"Can I call you mom, now? If you want?"

Like a strike of lightning in the dark, Laura's heart and mind leapt. She took a deep breath.

"Yes, that would be great, thanks."

That night they slept well, both happy, relieved and relaxed. With each day, they settled into a higher level of comfort and familiarity.

Jamella, comfortable and content in her room, drew colored sketches of animals, owls being her latest preoccupation past bedtime. The owls' feathers, beaks and eyes were detailed, lifelike. Jamella's talent was impressive. School art teachers encouraged formal lessons, but Jamella was not interested. The drawings were soothing, hypnotic, and for her sake only, best done in the silence of her room. Her use of the internet and social media was limited to research about what caught her eye:

owls, animals, clouds, or planets. In some ways, her interests were more boyish, a relief for Laura who had expected makeup, clothes and pop culture to be the next parental bridge to cross.

Laura did worry, though, about Jamella's shyness, hoping the attention to detail was due to an artist's passion and sensibility. Jamella, in order, drew Blue Jays, Black-eyed Susan's, chipmunks, rabbits and now, owls because she had heard a distinctive, long, low hoot from the woods behind their home.

On weekends, Laura and Jamella would sit on the back porch bundled together in warm blankets sharing a set of binoculars and searching treetops for the bird late into the night. While it was pleasant to sit in the moonlight, Jamella's obsession surprised Laura. She knew little of Jamella's parents, other than what she had already learned from the social worker and the girl's file. Jamella's introspective, quiet behavior had remained the same during her time with Laura. She was easy to care for, never demanding or disrespectful.

Her only bad habit was to share her thoughts without a filter, which sometimes rubbed others wrong. Unfortunately, Jamella was the sad reality of drug addiction and neglect and came to Laura with no sense of who the girl might be or become so Laura worried.

"It's okay," Mary had said. "No child comes with a manual, right?"

With no markers to guide her, Laura brooded about being a good parent for Jamella, aware she was a white mother with a black-brown-skinned daughter. Laura was a planner and liked to be ready for whatever the girl might want or need. She knew bringing Jamella into her tidy, white professional accounts payable life would be a challenge, but the urge to be a parent and to share and feel love was what Laura needed, with or without a man.

So, at the age of thirty-six, Laura decided to stop waiting for a relationship miracle and became a foster parent, never thinking she would want to keep the first child to enter her world, and now here she was trying to stop her daughter's searching of the woods and get her off to bed.

"I heard it!" Jamella said, hoping for a few more minutes on the cold March night.

Instead of insisting on ending their evening, Laura wondered, "Why owls?"

"They're *wise*, "Jamella said with the "duh!" implied. "And pretty."

"Like you."

"No, I'm not. My hair's frizzy. I have bug eyes, freckles..."

"And you have a bedtime, too. Let's go."

Later, while lying on a cozy white comforter, Jamella watched the woods that rose gradually to an elevated meadow of long, dry grass flattened by snow and cold. The occasional passing car would light the naked trees, and Jamella saw for the first time the outline of an old wooden barn sitting on the edge of the field.

Too excited to sleep, she lifted the window sash, cold air sharpening her interest. Jamella crawled onto the porch roof, careful to place one foot in front of the other upon the angled, frosted asphalt. A barn, she thought, the perfect spot to find an owl.

2

Widower Frank "Skip" Lowell's Sunday morning began the same way by filling an empty cardboard box with the beer cans and bottles littered on his front lawn, then driving down the road in his 2004, blue manual transmission Ford Ranger to attend the ten o'clock Catholic mass in the rural town of Harmony.

A retired draftsman, he liked the straight lines of routine and never missed church service. Now, at seventy-nine years of age, he allowed more time for collecting cans, discarded plastic water bottles, and for handwashing. Placing the truck key in the ignition was a challenge. His right hand shook from an essential tremor requiring a bit of concentration and luck to start the pick-up. The shaking forced his retirement at sixty-seven from Reliant Engineering, his first and only job.

Once, his fingertips, pencil and paper acted with a gentle sense of intimacy and accomplishment. Some men used their hands to cut trees down, drive backhoes, paint houses or hold cell phones for a living, but Skip had drawn neat, clean lines while seated at an immaculately tidy draftsman's table and loved it.

The tremor had snuck up on him, his right hand twitching against his leg as he watched the televised evening news.

Soon, it became a chore to raise a glass of water or draw the straight lines for a schematic drawing.

In retirement, though, he hadn't missed his colleagues. His focus had always been on drawing and the slight scratch of pencil to paper, not on his co-workers. It was as if they weren't there.

He did miss, though, how the randomness of drawn lines became something. Upon retirement, he tried tying trout flies expecting the magnifier and light to help, but it wasn't his eyes or brain that betrayed him, just the thin fingers of his right hand and he adjusted.

Skip left his back door unlocked so he wouldn't have to stand in the cold and fumble with a key, and he threw away anything with buttons, but zippers were manageable with extra concentration. He used deep, wide bowls for soup or serving dog food to Ace, his white-whiskered black lab, and porcelain mugs he half-filled for coffee. Velcro secured sneakers and large numbers on his—*where the hell is the damn thing!*—cell phone were required.

Skip could hear well, glad not to strain to follow the new priest's sermon, who did speak loudly, as someone with youthful vigor would. He was resigned to the adjustments he had made not only to the tremor, but also to Eloise's death at the age of sixty, the result of a wrong-way driver on an interstate highway.

Eloise and their granddaughter, ten-year-old Libby, were on their way to school one morning and neither survived the crash.

Skip never reconciled how nineteen-year-old Lucia Martinez, after leaving her normal factory night shift, could confuse the on and off ramps on a road she traveled many times, even if she had shared a beer or two with a few co-workers after quitting time. Cited for driving under the influence, she was charged with two counts of vehicular manslaughter and sentenced to twenty years in prison. His son, John, was inconsolable.

"It should've been me," he said tearfully, "not Mom. I was out late after golf . . . just wanted to sleep in."

Carol, John's wife, said nothing, exhausted after the wake, while Skip sat slumped in a chair by the closed casket, unable to grieve.

How did she make that mistake?

Skip's draftsman's eye traced the clean lines and perfectly rounded oak casket corners to the brass pallbearer's handles and for a dreamy, dazed second forgot his loss.

"So many came to pay their respects," the lanky funeral home director said. "Would you like me to call a car service?"

Carol shook her head.

"No thanks," she said, helping Skip to his feet.

In the several weeks that followed, the three dined together every other night at Skip's during the week and on weekends at John's. Parishioners from Holy Family Catholic Church brought food and pastries, stopping by to express their condolences and offer support but never staying long.

Unfortunately, their kind words melded into an iron-heavy weight upon his chest, each visit leaving Skip flustered and winded.

Somewhere, too, within those vacant weeks, the inflating pressure of loss upon John and Carol fractured and split them apart, so Skip ate alone.

"We weren't doing so hot before," John said, "and losing Libby, well . . ."

"Oh," Skip said, dazed, cellphone having sunk into his neck.

He had assumed they were doing as well as could be expected. It was part of his straight-line, symmetric plan for life—marriage, family, work, then death. He never imagined a separation, or divorce.

"I won't be around as much, either, Dad. Took a sales job covering the whole northeast, but I'll stop by when I can."

"Okay," Skip said, the last word he would speak to his son for weeks.

In time, solitude became Skip's companion, while boozy self-medication cushioned the pressure upon John's soul.

Their lives took ever-widening trajectories, and one wondered less and less about the other. A new job for John and a reclusive life for Skip allowed for some untethering from tragedy, but like a dark stranger, it cast a shadow upon them. The "excuse me" ...tap-tap upon their souls was always within reach and while John floundered, oftentimes passed out drunk in a motel on the road, Skip placed one foot in front of the other upon a line that never wobbled.

Eloise was gone, but the house remained as she had fashioned it, even after the window drapes had faded and thinned from the sun of many days.

Sugar spoiled, while cinnamon and flour hardened in canisters left untouched in the pantry. Dust and dog hair clung together under furniture and to the faded leather of Eloise's sneakers waiting by the back door. The once shiny oak floor near the threshold was dabbled with paw and shoe prints. It was Skip's job to sweep the floor, his part in the hum of long-time couples and the shared duet of chores.

She did the wash, but Skip did the bedsheets. Eloise shoveled the walk while Skip did the driveway, and he cooked little or mostly not at all.

He ate oatmeal or dry cereal for breakfast with peanut butter, hot dogs, canned soups and stews or, occasionally, fast food mid-afternoon, his last meal of the day. He drank cups of black coffee and finished the evening with a bottle of pilsner, usually while sitting in the barn.

The afternoons were still dark in March, so Skip carried a flashlight out to the field to find Cal, his twenty-five-year-old, still black as night, Arabian horse. He led it into the stable and sat on a bale of hay watching as the horse he had bought for Libby and taught her how to ride, chewed its dinner. To his left hung the saddle and tack, leather dried and cracked.

Over the years, he had used the hay and manure for Eloise's garden, but now it lay in clumps behind the barn, a warm home for mice, chipmunks and rabbits.

Ace, having sniffed about the corners of the barn, now lay at Skip's feet. The beer made his eyelids heavy and he drifted off, chin on his chest. He would wake an hour before midnight to find Jamella standing in the barn, mouth wide-open.

3

She had wandered through the open barn door, eyes trained upon the wooden rafters made visible by the long beam of a flashlight.

Ace raised his head, but the old man snored softly, unaware of the girl.

Jamella's mind focused on the tantalizing thought of finding an owl. She methodically checked each crossbeam, hoping to find straw and twig nests, and noting the sullen, hidden face poses of brown bats hanging from the rear peak.

The horse neighed and Jamella jumped.

"Oh," she said, dropping the beam of light to Skip's feet. "Awesome!" she said of the horse, its dark muscled legs and neck sharpened in the shadows of half-light.

Ace barked, and Jamella stepped back.

Skip's eyes opened, then closed from the pierce of light.

"Who are you?" Jamella asked. "Does your dog bite?"

Skip, mind fogged by booze and sleep said reflexively, "Who's asking?"

"Me. Jamella. Is that your horse?"

Skip took in the sight of a brown, thin-boned girl, dark eyes lit with reflected light.

"Why are you in my barn?" he said, his mind coming alive. "You're looking to steal something, aren't you?"

He stood quickly, his height at six-foot three, surprised Jamella.

Skip's flannel jacket hung from bony shoulders like it was held in place with hidden clothespins. He took three stooped paces but stopped when Laura burst through the door.

"What the hell is all this?" Skip said.

He stared at Laura, her curly black hair dangling from underneath a wool cap. She wore a gray vinyl jacket half zipped around a full waist.

Laura, her flannel pajama pants ruffled and bunched into the top of untied vinyl boots said, "Jamella! What on earth?"

The girl, eyes fixed on the raven-black Arabian with its ears perked and nostrils wide, didn't reply. She moved to the horse, its head high upon its shoulders, neck muscles long and sleek.

"Are you responsible for this?" Skip asked, thinking it had been a long time since he carried a shotgun to the barn.

"Yes. Uh, no. Jamella!" Laura said. "Let's go."

"I didn't know there was a horse," Jamella said softly to herself. "How did you find me?"

"The flashlight, obviously," Laura said, exasperated. "That and the cold air from the open window in your room."

Skip turned on the overhead light, expecting the girl to move, to leave, but she stood with mouth open, the flashlight shining on the stray bits of hay stuck into the black laces of her leather sneakers.

Dream-like, she turned her eyes to Skip and Ace.

"Who are you?" Jamella asked.

"Jamella, please," Laura said, taking the girl by arm. "So sorry. She was looking for owls."

"We live down the hill behind the barn," Jamella said, as she walked with her mother.

Skip, sure he'd never laid eyes on them, said, "No you don't. That's Simpson's place."

"It was," Laura said. "I bought it—estate sale—four years ago."

Skip shook his head.

"Estate sale?" he said, "No, I just saw him."

"The guy's obviously dead," Jamella said, her left thumb pointing to the dirt.

"Sorry again. Good night," Laura said, walking Jamella by the scruff of her jacket into the darkness.

Skip, Ace and Cal stood, eyes fixed on the wide barn exit and the shadowy night sky. Had they witnessed phantoms? True, he had not seen old man Simpson walking his beagle in a long time...but four years?

"Hmm," Skip said. "What do you make of that? White woman with a black kid. Anything goes, I guess."

He threw a thin cotton blanket over Cal's back, secured its two straps, patted the horse's neck, then left with Ace alongside. He considered installing a padlock on the door, but he would struggle with the key. God forbid a fire, too, would doom the horse. He hoped to never see the girl again but wasn't sure.

"If she shows up again, Ace, I'll scare her off good."

He stood behind the barn, watching the lights from Laura's house flick on and off as she and Jamella moved from room to room.

Ed Simpson was a retired electrician who Skip had called to replace a kitchen outlet or a worn breaker. A white van, usually parked by a tool shed, was gone, as were its tire track ruts in the grass. Ed's place had a new roof and clean beige vinyl siding.

Skip stood with Ace, the dog pressed against the front of the old man's legs. The lights inside the house went off, and a lonely owl hooted. Time, he thought, moved like the wind.

4

Jamella had hardly slept. In her mind the horse, man, and dog appeared like a still photograph. The barn was cold, smelled of hay and manure, but it was the horse and its shiny blackness that would not leave her. Instinctively, she traced the horse's neck and head with a finger against her thigh over and over. She rose, grabbed her sketchpad and worked by the window well into the night.

In the morning, Laura called twice to Jamella but didn't hear the girl's footsteps upon the second floor hall to the bathroom.

Jamella slept with her head under a pillow and with three drawings of the horse scattered among the blankets. Laura was not worried about sending her to school with less than a good night's sleep. Jamella functioned well on uneven rest.

With the touch of Laura's hand upon her shoulder, Jamella sat up, rubbed her eyes and said, "That horse, wow, what's its name?"

Laura sighed. She knew another visit to the barn was unavoidable.

Pulling black leggings and a light-pink shirt from a painted white dresser drawer, Jamella continued, "Not sure if it's a boy horse or not, could you tell? I think it's a boy...might be. How cool would it be if it's a girl? I liked the dog, too. Didn't bark or bite. The old guy's weird, though. What was he doing just sitting there in the dark? I mean, who does that?"

"Jamella."

"I couldn't see anything at all. Why sit in the dark?"

"Jamella!"

At breakfast, thankfully, the girl ate quietly. She didn't like when crumbs flew out of her mouth, either, which gave Laura a chance to explain that it wasn't their barn or property.

"And why would you sneak out of the house? Do you know how dangerous that is?"

"I just decided to go. Sorry," Jamella said, head down. "I should've asked first."

"No kidding," she said, patting Jamella's hand. "We'll stop by later and you're going to apologize," she said, and Jamella nodded, demonstrating shame, but hiding the thrill of returning to the barn.

The ride to school in Laura's red Nissan SUV was unusually quiet with Jamella staring out the back seat passenger's side window, lost in thought.

Laura hoped she was thinking of the mistake she had made so she said, "Jamella, trespassing is something that I can't protect you from, do you understand?"

The girl nodded, but her eyes were wide, vacant.

"If you get in trouble with the police, there are adult consequences, like reform school. You know what that is, right?" and at that a chill rose in Laura's chest.

Child services could take her!

Turning into the parent drop-off queue, Laura regained her composure.

She looked at Jamella through the rearview mirror and the girl said, "Yeah, I know. It's a prison for kids. Sort of like the group homes I was in, but not as bad."

Jamella lifted the door handle.

"I'll apologize," she said. "Because he's a sad man," and with a whoosh the car door closed behind her.

Jamella walked along the cement walkway, eyes looking down, as she hastily navigated through the happy chatter of other children.

Laura accelerated from the curb, wondering if three and a half years was proof enough to child services of her capability as a parent, even when Laura herself was unsure. Managing a successful, small bookkeeping company demonstrated her reliability, but being a parent was always new. Laura was one to overthink, so she chided herself to stop worrying. She'd march Jamella over to the old man and have her apologize as a good parent should, and hopefully, that would be the end of it.

Off and on during the day, Jamella and Laura would think about Skip. Laura hoped he'd be reasonable, while Jamella wondered how she had never noticed the old man and his impressive horse.

Did he hide it on purpose?

Jamella sensed sadness, too, for the old man slumped and asleep on a bale of hay with the tired dog at his feet, while the horse was as alert as a prisoner hoping to be free.

Or maybe, Jamella thought, the horse was lonely like she was with no one of its kind for company. Unlike owls, or any of the animals she had chased, only the horse had acknowledged the girl. Its glossy, black plaintive eyes locked onto hers.

She felt a deep stirring of excitement and joy, which made keeping up with her lessons impossible. She would smile for no reason or care little for the trifles of the others. The warmth in her belly and the racing of her brain was more than the excitement she had experienced when she was adopted and realized she would have a permanent home—and bedroom—of her own!

The school day could not end fast enough. Jamella would be polite and hope the old man would let her see the horse again. He had to or Jamella would lose her mind.

Once home, she raced from the school bus, through the back door and up the stairs to her room.

Laura, from the driveway, noticed the back door wide open and Jamella's jacket and backpack on the floor.

Jamella came hopping down the stairs, two at a time, with drawings of the Arabian in her hand.

"I'll give him these," she said. "He'll like them."

"I hadn't planned on going now," Laura said to no one, as Jamella was already in the backyard, black and lime striped sneakers barely touching the frozen grass.

5

"Let's be smart about this," Laura said, standing atop the hill, the barn and house before them. "We don't want to upset the man."

Jamella spotted the Arabian by the tree line, its nose to the ground, tail waving slightly in the breeze. Wood rails were nailed to square posts along the length and width of a football field, accessed by a gate a short distance from the back door of the house.

The Arabian was free to roam from the barn, which made Jamella smile, but she was surprised by the drab, stained cotton blanket strapped to it for warmth.

"Can we buy the horse a new blanket?" she asked.

"It's not our horse," Laura said, "and be polite. That sounds like an insult."

"Maybe he's too poor."

"I doubt it," Laura said, looking at the expansive property, which though, showed its age.

The bungalow had porches in the front and rear with pale, white peeling shingles and curled black roof tiles.

Weather beaten, Laura thought, as were the vertical plank barn boards, some warped and pried from the frame, nails loose and rusted.

The pickup parked in the yard had some rot on the door panels. A wire garden fence stood in waves, some of it flattened under leaves and long grass, while the rest still stood attached to rusting, green steel rods driven into the soil, straining to stay upright.

Inside the house, Ace barked, the deep baritone rumbling within the walls.

The horse looked, sniffed, then continued nipping at the cold earth.

Laura handed Jamella the store bought coffee cake, "Remember, let's be polite."

She pressed the doorbell, but it made no sound.

Skip came to the door's half window, his shadowy image sliding a faded, cotton curtain to one side.

"What do *you* want?" he asked, impatiently.

Laura said, "We wanted to apologize for last night."

She waited for the door to open, or for the old man to speak, but he stood silent.

"My daughter has a cake for you. Thought you might like it."

Skip shook his head, "Your daughter?"

Laura nodded.

"No husband?"

Flustered, Laura said, "What? No."

"I'm adopted," Jamella said loudly. She moved closer. "Can I see the horse again?"

"No," he said firmly.

"Come on," Laura said to Jamella. "We'll leave the cake."

"Don't want it."

"Sorry I scared you," Jamella said, as Laura pulled her by the sleeve.

Skip leaned into the glass, left brown eye cold-focused on the girl.

"Don't come back here," he said.

Stunned, Laura stepped from the porch, the old man's heavy stare upon her.

She moved quickly, not noticing the car stopped by the house.

The car door opened and a crumpled white coffee cup fell onto the driveway, followed by a set of black sneakers and wrinkled, tan chino pant legs. Mud brown snow was caked upon the outside of the front fenders.

Standing, the man said, "Did you just pop in to visit Frank?"

"Who?" Jamella said.

"Right. Or Skip. That's what most people call him. I'm John, his son."

"Laura and Jamella...neighbors," Laura said, cheeks red with frustration. "We just stopped by for a second."

"He was mean," Jamella said. "I just wanted to see the horse. And I made these for him," Jamella said, holding out the three rolled drawings.

John pressed his lips together.

Nodding, he said, "Dad can be a grouch, sorry. Can I see those?"

John unfolded each drawing carefully, gently placing them against the warm metal hood of the car. His eyes widened.

"That's Cal," he said, "for sure. You're very good."

"That's the horse's name?"

"Yup. My daughter named him Blackie but," John cleared his throat, "Cal suits him. Cal Ripken played for the Baltimore Orioles and never wanted to leave the field."

He raised his cloudy green eyes to watch the horse walking toward the barn.

Must be his mother's eyes, Laura thought.

"But that was a long time ago. So, do you take art lessons?"

"She doesn't."

"Can I see Cal?' Jamella asked, bouncing up and down on her toes. "Like up close?"

"Why not? Let me check with my dad. If you wait by the gate, Cal will come over to you."

John took the drawings to the house.

Frank waited behind the door. He opened it just as John raised a fist to knock.

"What are you doing?" Skip hissed.

"Checking in," John said casually. "You told them to leave?"

"Yes, I did. Don't want kids around here. Once you let one visit, you know how it is, you get a run of them wanting to ride."

They stood, the kitchen table covered with a white plastic sheet embossed with a tiny red rooster print, between them. The room was as he remembered. The green Formica countertop had faded and was worn near the toaster and coffee pot. The clunky sounding black refrigerator wobbled when it ran. The white porcelain sink had dark circles by the drains. Between the knobs of the gas oven, a small clock ticked off seconds, its slight hand shakily cataloging infinity.

If only it were a magic wand, John thought, so I could wish back the last twenty years, a do-over, a mulligan.

"You know you're holding a shotgun, Dad, right?"

The old man's hard white knuckles held the handle and barrel. His arms, once solid and thick, were thin and slack. His voice, too, was softer, almost dry.

"I keep one by each door. You never know."

"Sure. Bet you get some rough customers here. Is that a new habit?"

Skip shrugged.

"Just putting them to use when needed."

"Why don't you leave that and come outside. Nice woman, and the daughter made these for you. Pretty good, I'd say."

Skip placed the gun by the coat rack. With a wad of tissue, he shakily wiped away the spit from the side of his mouth.

He said, "Didn't know you were coming."

Waiting for a reply, he noted the smooth skin and thick brown hair his son got from Eloise. He was her son, with her soft eyes and patience.

John opened the door and Ace scooted through the crack.

"That's because you don't answer the phone. Say something nice about the drawings."

Laura stood with Jamella and Cal, the girl on tiptoes, hand over the gate, petting the horse's nose, talking loudly.

"Yes, I know. It's beautiful," Laura repeated to her excited child.

Skip grunted.

"Now you've done it. She'll want to come by all the time."

"There's something about that horse, Dad," John said. "Hard not to love."

Ace jumped, knocking the cake box from Laura's hand. "Sorry," John said, "Thought Ace was too old to get excited."

"Don't let him eat that," Skip said, as Ace pawed at the closed cover.

Laura grabbed the box and the dog stood on its hind legs, front paws onto the woman's chest.

"Here, Ace," John said, grabbing the dog's collar.

To his father he said, "Don't you feed him?"

"Sure. Cheap stuff," Skip said, and John smiled.

"I'm Laura. And this pest is Jamella."

"Like peanut butter and Jamella," the girl said. "I get that a lot at school. Why were you sitting in the dark?"

"Jamella," Laura said, "That's none of your—"

"Old Cal can be a slow eater," John said.

"Sorry, *again*. It's just that when she gets something in her head, there's no stopping her."

"That's not a bad quality," John said. Good for a sales."

"Got no discipline, huh?" Skip said.

"Dad, please."

"Sometimes," Jamella said, "I have a problem with my brain."

"What?" Laura said. "Who says that?"

"It's okay, Mom. I can handle it." Jamella said. "I'm going to help you with the horse, okay?"

"I don't think so," Skip said. "Visiting time is over."

"Your hand shakes, that's not good."

"We should go," Laura said, tugging the girl's arm. "Nice to meet you."

Walking briskly, Laura admonished her daughter. "Don't just say what's in your head. You have to think of how people feel."

"But his hand does shake *a lot.*"

"I'm sure he knows that. Why remind him he's not okay?"

"I'm not okay and it's not a big deal."

Jamella easily hopped from foot to foot down the hill, leaving her mother behind.

Standing at the back door of their home, cold wind slid down from the sloped embankment and around their legs.

Laura said, "So what's wrong with you?"

"We don't have any friends. That's not okay, is it?"

But Jamella didn't wait for a reply. She walked into the kitchen leaving Laura in the backyard, standing amidst the first swirling flakes of a snow squall.

"We're too busy," she said defensively, knowing it was an excuse.

She sighed but was glad to have broken the ice with her neighbor.

6

"Brought you a present," John said, holding an answering machine. "If you insist on keeping a landline, and not keeping your cell charged, then you need this."

Skip sat at the kitchen table rubbing the cold from his fingers. Outside, the wind and snow intensified.

Cal would have made his way into the barn by now, he thought. He imagined the horse, head bowed, hooves thumping the frozen earth as he walked to a narrow side doorway left open inside the corral.

"Smart," he said of Cal.

John, kneeling and reaching for the electrical wall socket behind the living room couch said, "Thanks."

Normally, Skip would have added "ass" to smart but skipped the dig at his son. Instead, he watched John move purposefully, swinging wires around and behind the end table.

Ace sat near John, waiting, ears perked, tail swishing over the floor.

"After four rings the machine kicks in. A light flashes if there's a message."

Skip nodded.

"I know how they work."

John appeared thinner in the dark shadows cast by the snowy clouds, his green eyes steady like soft light from a dark hallway.

Eloise.

"What happened to the other one? It die on you?" John said, standing straight with his dad's full height, hands on hips.

Skip sighed, the air awkwardly still.

It die on you?

No, it hadn't died, just placed in the trash, for Skip was exhausted by well-meaning phone calls. Honestly, how many times could he say he was fine?

"I've got news," John said. "Got a promotion. No more road grind. Work a bit from home, too, along with a good raise."

Skip vaguely remembered John's work to be with medical supplies but had not asked in so long he wasn't sure.

"What company?" he said, hoping the name would reveal his son's field, but when John replied it was at the same place, Skip's mind went blank, slick and shiny like an empty office whiteboard.

He was forgetting, too, trash pickup day, or when he had last checked for mail at the post office. In the morning, he sometimes found a room light shining, or the blue-flame gas stove burner hissing like a cornered snake.

Occasionally, too, rain puddled on the floor by a drafty window, or an open refrigerator would cast a ghost-like presence into the kitchen.

Oddities, he first thought, but when they happened again, he made checklists to help. He created rules to follow like "turn flame off before removing frying pan", "flush before washing hands", and "fill Ace's water dish before making coffee". They were his rules for living alone.

"Did you get the notice," John asked, "from the Bureau of Corrections?"

He lifted the neat pile of mail sitting on the coffee table.

"This one," he said of the unopened envelope. "Martinez served her time. Want to read it?"

"Nope," he said with a shake of his head.

John sat on the couch, envelope in hand.

"Don't blame you. Tired of getting these, too, but she at least served pretty much the full sentence. Just like we have, huh?"

He ran his fingers along the clean, strong edges of the official letter, thinking of the parole hearings. They learned Lucia was a model prisoner, working on a Certified Nurses' Assistant certificate, and was genuinely sorry for her actions.

John and Skip, who spoke in support of Libby and Eloise, left meetings frustrated and spent.

After the first parole hearing, John said, "I don't care if she was on suicide watch or that she's rehabilitating herself. Isn't that what she's supposed to do? Geez, they tell us stuff like we should care...like we're *her* parents!"

But haunted by the ghost of his own selfishness the *if only I had been driving* whispers that came to him at night in empty motel rooms, or over long, drowsy stretches of highway, returned. So many thoughts of how he would have been quicker to react, or how he might have left home earlier—or later—with Libby, a second either way or they would not have crashed, been obliterated.

Every two years, an official letter arrived and every two years, John's stomach turned to stone.

He hated Lucia, whose narrow shoulders, soft voice, and tears upon her round cheeks reminding him of the moment his heart stopped, his mind spun, and despair pulled his life into a deep, airless tomb.

Eventually, he and his father would miss the last three parole hearings.

Lucia was now a grown woman, her release inevitable, while a smiling mother, wife, and easy-going daughter were forever lost.

The prison meetings were frustrating revisits of stolen hopes, loves and futures, which left them exhausted and twisted into straightjackets of helplessness.

When his father surprisingly recounted for the parole board how, on the day of his seventieth birthday Skip had fallen from a ladder, John knew they'd never return.

Skip, when he spoke to the board, usually repeated how he missed "his happy little Libby" and "his good wife, Eloise." At the last hearing, though, he softly retold how he had slipped while cleaning a gutter, fell from a ladder, and had landed flat on his back. In pain and struggling to breathe, Skip rolled onto his side, wondering if he had broken ribs. His attention shifted to Ace, who nuzzled against Skip's shoulder and to Cal, standing by the fence. In the distance, the afternoon sun flashed off the fluttering red and yellow maple leaves at the tree line. Above it, pillow-white clouds moved along the deep, endless blue horizon.

Skip said, "I'd be better off now if I could join my wife and granddaughter."

He paused, and the room with its high ceilings and dark, wainscoted walls, quieted beyond hearing.

Finally, a woman from the board said with a slight smile, "But you do, at least, have your son," causing those in the room—Lucia, Carol, Jesus, Lucia's brother, and two other hearing officers—to shuffle or clear their throats.

"At the *very* least," John scoffed, his words filling the room.

Lucia squeezed her hands together. With tears rimming her eyes, she said, "I never meant this."

"But here we are," John said, angrily. "Thanks to you."

As time passed, John decided societal laws, rules, and redemption were for suckers, fools, romantics, and nothing loved and lost was ever made whole. He would continue to straddle along the edges of living, oftentimes wondering why he bothered.

He had met other women, dated a few, but didn't commit. Like something was caught in his throat, he could not say the right words, or sound convincing or sincere, and his relationships trailed off.

So, no, why would his dad want to read, "Dear Sir/Madam: Please be advised that inmate number 777871FO32, Lucia G. Martinez, will be officially released from incarceration on Friday, March 15th, 2019, having completed the terms set forth by the State Legislature for the crime of vehicular homicide resulting in death," when nothing for either of them would change? It was just another letter to clutter one's mailbox, take up one's time, and require energy to open then trash—the cycle of anticipation, disappointment, and déjà vu of everyday life. The Dear Sir/Madam decorum of the rational world, obliterated in a flash of chaos, made what was fair and just an illusion.

They sat in the living room, Skip watching the local television news, John watching Skip and thinking of how his father handled grief.

Skip put one foot in front of the other, his tough-skinned attitude a remnant of his early years of service as a platoon leader during the Vietnam War. He respected his father's stoicism, but John struggled.

Alcohol let him sleep and offered a life raft when the tide of pain rose around him, but the hurt and self-hate lingered.

One late afternoon, while driving on a country road, John decided to end it all, but a child straddling a bike by a telephone pole saved him.

He had successfully closed on a major new account, one that would add significantly to his end-of-year bonus but instead of being happy, sadness overwhelmed him as he thought of the empty motel room and the bottle of Beefeater awaiting his return. As he imagined the worn carpet, rust stained toilet, and half-open suitcase, he couldn't picture Libby's face. With the car radio turned off, he tried harder, but her smiling eyes were gone.

"Libby?" he said.

He had wondered many times at what point in life did nothing matter?

And he'd reached that moment.

With tears running down his cheeks, unending pain empowered him. He pressed the accelerator and the car jolted forward. In the evening shadows, a utility pole stood above the low tree line, and he aimed for it. Relief at leaving the world he had shadow-walked disguised as a happy man calmed him. The futility of living gave way to the peace of dying.

It was time.

Ahead, a young girl with a lime green bicycle between her legs came into sight as she waited to cross the two-lane highway. Holding a hand to her eyes to shield herself from the on-coming headlamps, she stood, late for home.

John spotted two red reflector lights, and a bright white tee shirt. His brain sharply woke.

Stunned, John swerved from the shoulder of the road while pushing the brake pedal. The girl, unaware, watched as John drove past, bits of gravel spinning from the tires' treads and scattering around her.

Heart thumping, he stopped by the side of the road.

"God!" he said, taking his shaking hands from the wheel.

When he looked to see if she had crossed safely, there was no sign of her.

John sat, waiting for his breathing to settle, while sweat beaded against his shirt collar. Instead of feeling anger and shame over a moment of selfishness that had almost taken an innocent life, he felt relief. Was the girl by the side of the road Libby? He eventually believed so.

John was not superstitious or religious but was now convinced Libby had been on the road with him.

The how or why of it didn't matter.

Over time, he felt a renewed responsibility to live a life she would be proud of so he stopped drinking and kept active. Before the silence of an empty home could tempt him to sip from a glass of gin and tonic, he would lace on a pair of sneakers and walk, preferring dark, shadowy lit pavements to occupy his mind. With a sweatshirt hood pulled over his head, he embraced the darkness. Except for a passing car or two, he was alone, his thoughts free.

What might have been—a wife, daughter, and possible grandchild—was a fate from which the hypnotic patter of worn-soled sneakers took the sting. John would return to his condominium apartment, shower, and then grab whatever deli salad or sandwich cooled in the refrigerator.

Heartache had become madness, but Libby saved him.

He was surprisingly content, too, to sit now with his father and cozy up to what family he had.

For years, John thought little of Skip or of the house in which he had once lived, remarkable in how nothing had changed, time seemingly forever still.

Skip was not one for chitchat, but John, interested in his father's experiences asked, "Dad, how have you handled Mom and Libby being gone all these years?"

At first, John suspected his father had not heard him, but the old man stirred.

He said, "When I was a kid, ten maybe, I watched a man in a three-piece suit jump in front of a moving train."

Surprised by this revelation—John had expected to learn of his father's daily habits and routines—he leaned forward.

"We were in dad's station wagon at a railroad crossing, waiting. The guy ran on foot and bang!"

Skip smacked a fist into his palm.

"Gone, like that. Just disappeared. Saw it first hand, too, in the service. No surprise by then. But I kept going, GI bill, work, your mother, you, family."

"I never heard that one," John said, wondering how a ten year-old is affected by witnessing the violent suicide of a stranger.

"Never had a reason to tell it," he said casually.

"Did it bother you?"

"Nah. I was too young, but it did later when I was in Vietnam. It's sure easy to lose hope."

"How about now? Still going to church?"

"Yup, don't want to be on His bad side."

Skip paused.

The connecting rooms were black, funereal.

He continued, "And it's been my time for a while now. I got everything set with the lawyer—even marked out four house lots of land you could sell. Over on the other corner where those damn kids drink and smoke marijuana. He'll notify you when the time comes."

John stood with a smile on his face, thinking of the times he drank and smoked there, too.

Patting Skip's shoulder he said, "That's good, but you're not going anywhere. This furniture, though, ought to go. Smells like the barn in here."

"That's my cologne."

Jamella sat upon the soft blue carpet in her room, staring at a large, blank sheet of artist's newsprint paper, when the slide of Laura's slippers stopped at the door.

Her parental sense nagged her. She could not let her daughter think they were friendless, but the girl was right. Being single, she had fallen from the radar of married couples and, when she was with them, their domestic lives were fuller than hers. She found herself "liking" Facebook posts more often than sitting with friends. Work was work, which she enjoyed, and nothing much changed. Her parents and two sisters had welcomed Jamella to the family, but beyond an occasional visit, her sisters, too, led full, married lives and slid away.

That's it, Laura thought, Jamella's cousins could be friends.

She asked, "Do you want me to invite Jody or Leah over this weekend? Maybe both?"

Jamella lifted her wide, dreamy eyes to Laura.

"No," she said simply, the idea deflating.

Laura did not insist. Actually, it wasn't the best idea since the girls would have to take a bus ride on a Friday after school to spend the weekend with Jamella. Instead, she watched as Jamella waved her left hand over the paper, making imaginary lines. Not having any skill with drawing or art, she watched the process play out.

Jamella sat back on her legs, arms folded.

"I'm having trouble with this," she said, finally. "The old man. I can't see him."

"Oh? You mean, like details?"

"No. I know what he looks like, but I don't like what I see. His eyes are so like, confusing."

"He *is* grumpy."

"Then he needs a friend. He can be mine."

Laura leaned against the doorjamb.

"I don't think so. You're better off spending Saturday with your cousins."

Jamella shook her head.

"No. Don't ask them. It's too weird and awkward. They treat me like I'm a puppy or a toy. Plus, they'd be ticked off if you made them come from far away. I know I wouldn't like to do that."

"Maybe if they came over more, you'd feel different about it."

Jamella stood.

"They're not like me. They take music lessons and go to gymnastics, yuck."

Yes, they were unalike, but by Jamella's choosing. She had an introvert's shyness, the fear of taking a step like a skater on thin ice. Jamella was right, though, about the awkwardness.

Laura had sensed her father thinking when she decided to adopt, if *this*, a biracial child is what makes you happy, fine. Still, the disappointment of choosing Jamella over a family of her own floated near the surface. Or did she imagine it?

Her parents were open armed and helpful, but there was no hugging Jamella like the other grandchildren. Jamella was more prickly than cuddly. Laura ignored these thoughts at family gatherings, watching as Jamella reluctantly and haltingly interacted with others, even when they expressed interest in her art, her teachers, or clothes.

Laura would say that Jamella was doing well, not wanting to admit Jamella was strong-willed, intense, and maybe developing learning problems at school.

The most she would say about Jamella's reticence was, jokingly, "My daughter's a minimalist," hoping Jamella wouldn't become the problem child of the family.

Laura reminded herself, too, that Jamella wasn't an ordinary girl or that theirs was an ordinary family. It would take time to sort itself.

"Your attitude could be a little better," Laura said with encouragement. "If you tried, you could have lots of friends."

"I *do* try . . . sometimes."

Jamella turned her face from her mother.

"But kids think I'm weird."

Laura wrapped her arms around Jamella, hugging her thin back, while listening to the girl's stifled sighs.

"What about the girl on the bus? Why not ask her to come over?"

"Hannah's my school friend, and she's really quiet. She just likes to read and hang at home."

Laura nodded, thinking that maybe she could arrange a time for Hannah to visit on the weekend.

In an attempt to cheer her daughter, she said, "I have to work on my attitude, too," Laura said of her empty social calendar, or of the possibility of a partner.

"I am going to see the horse again," Jamella said, "but not at night."

"Good," Laura said with a laugh. "I'm not up for another midnight hike in the cold."

She turned Jamella's face to hers.

"We can work together on making a new friend, how's that? Won't be easy, though."

Jamella returned to the blank paper, pencil in hand.

"I'll think of something," she said. "What do horses like to eat?"

"Carrots, I think."

The next day, John left the office early to rent a rug shampooer. Normally, he had cared little about the condition of his childhood home, but his father's frailty and shadowy isolation lingered with John long after he had left Skip the night before. His dad was officially old and had been for a while, his stooped walk and shaking hand a flashing sign to a son who had been distant, distracted. It was time now to do more, offer help and, in the case of the earthy smelling furniture, dirty curtains, and peeling paint, not take no for an answer.

It was another rehabilitative step for a son who had drifted, consumed with sadness, loss, and gin.

While waiting for the clerk at the hardware store, John felt happy, empowered, and purposeful.

The local police Sergeant, Ed Wilson, who had been a high school friend, recognized John. They reconnected, Ed mindful of the car accident and not saying as much as he would like about his own wife and grown daughters, one about to have the family's first grandchild.

They spoke of parents, then Ed asked, "How's Skip's front yard? Still finding trash there on weekends?"

"I didn't know that. How long has it been going on?" John said.

"Since the state posted a no littering sign on the pole in front of the house. I told your dad I'd see what I could do."

Wilson's eyes suffered from the perpetual red-rimmed, watery effect of long overnight shifts and little sleep.

"I waited there for a bit on Friday night, but weekends are tough—domestic calls, drunks. But I'll keep trying, probably high school kids."

"He's never complained. Probably figures the police have more important things to do."

Wilson sighed.

"We do. Lots of affordable housing came in. There goes the neighborhood, right? Keeps us extra busy."

Laura Pel emerged from the backroom of the store dressed in gray work slacks, a white blouse, light gray pullover, and holding a briefcase.

"Nice to see you again," she said to John, her light brown eyes brightened by the noonday sunshine flooding the front of the store. Dark wisps of hair curled over a pencil seated snuggly behind her right ear.

"I know you," Wilson said. "You're the woman with the little bl—uh, girl. You bought the Simpson house. I helped them move. We met then."

"I remember. You can let them know we're happy with the house."

"I will. You handle income taxes, right?" Wilson asked. "Might need you this year. College deductions, I hope."

The police dispatcher's voice from the radio pinned to Wilson's shoulder interrupted them.

"Got to go," he said, stepping to the door.

"Let's have a beer," he said to John.

"Taxes, bookkeeping, that's your business?" John said. "Might need you, too."

"I don't know," Laura said, teasingly. "I'm popular in the spring, but my daughter loves that horse. Any way she can visit again?"

"Not my horse but, sure, I'll be there tomorrow by nine o'clock. Going to help my dad with some long overdue spring cleaning, like from 2004. Stop by."

7

er brother, Jesus, greeted Lucia as she walked with wobbly legs through the prison gates. It was a bright, warm, snow-melting March day, and she lifted her eyes to the sun.

"Finally," Jesus said, wrapping his arms around her. "Finally, finally. *Free.*"

She buried her head into the opening of his wool jacket and held tight. Relief, anxiety, and love for her brother, who visited Lucia every other week, choked her with emotion.

Her only brother, divorced with two teenagers, and who worked six days a week as a commercial painter, had never missed making the two-hour round-trip drive to the prison. With her nose against his work shirt, the smells of sweat, nicotine and paint thinner were mild and mixed. His chest was thin, but his arms were muscled, wiry.

"Mi *roca*," she mumbled, "my rock."

"Of course, Little Sister," Jesus said, his brown eyes and square chin like his father's. "We are family. Come. I have a surprise for you."

Waiting by a blue panel truck were Jesus' teenagers, Maria and Roberto. Lucia had seen many pictures of their first communions, days spent at the beach, soccer games, but as they stood bored and staring at their cellphones, Lucia knew them only as strangers.

"Put those away. This is your *Tia*, Lucia."

Dressed like their father in paint-blotched, gray work clothes, they smiled politely.

Roberto extended his right hand, and Lucia touched the boy she had never known in flesh and blood.

She blinked back tears.

Maria hugged her aunt lightly.

"Yes, this is good," Jesus said. "Time to go. We have reservations at a nice restaurant. Some real food on your first day."

Roberto and Maria climbed into the side of the van and sat on white plastic paint buckets.

Lucia, seated in the front, rested against the slightly open window, cool glass against her cheek. She wore the baggy jeans and an oversized cotton blouse Jesus had brought for her release, but was anxious to dig through the boxes of personal possessions Jesus had kept for her. With little money, she agreed to live in one of the tenement flats Jesus owned, report to the probation officer, and learn to paint while working with her brother. Her patient, kind brother.

Jesus teased that since she was released, maybe he could arrange a date for her? Surely, a gentleman would be more than willing to help her get back in the game.

Lucia's face reddened. She peaked at Roberto and Maria, but they wore earbuds, minds lost to music.

Softly, she said, "Thank you, but I can wait, unlike men."

Jesus laughed.

"Good. Better if you find one on your own. Some of the men I know," he said, hand extended, waving his thumb up then down like a skiff on the open ocean.

Lucia nodded. A man in her life would be nice someday.

As they turned onto the interstate, Jesus said, "Ah, the fresh air smells good, huh?"

Lucia only nodded, thinking instead of the trash she had picked up many times along the highway while working the prison work detail. The first few times, she had kept her back to the passing cars but, overtime, she was glad to be outside with no walls, no sour inmates looking to fight.

Cars had changed. They were bigger. There were more trucks and traffic, more coffee cups, cardboard, and plastic bags, too.

She'd been lucky to serve the majority of her sentence in minimum confinement, when she was later deemed not a threat to others or herself. She completed her high school diploma, and earned a certified nursing assistant's certificate. In time, she planned to attend college, something she would not have thought she was capable of when in high school.

She had been by her estimation a silly girl who was well-behaved and polite, but unfocused, more concerned with her girlfriends than her studies. Leaving school to work was not discouraged, though, because her parents worked as a landscaper and house cleaner, so the extra money helped.

Jesus, though, was the go-getter and she should have worked with him when he offered, but working with men in the trades required more self-confidence than she had. So, Lucia opted for factory work and set small, immediate goals, like buying a car.

It was the small celebration with a few work friends after their shift, standing beside a newly purchased 1994 red Dodge Colt that precipitated the accident.

As Lucia laughed and drank from a can of beer, she no longer felt like a teenager. After all, she had just turned nineteen and could sign her own papers, which she did by applying for a car loan.

Now she was fully realized, an adult, but the giddy moment of satisfaction ended with an explosion of metal that left her concussed. She also suffered from a fractured right leg and three broken ribs.

Alive and floating on a wave of pain medication, she was arraigned in the hospital, only to remember Jesus say, "We need a lawyer, Little Sister," and wondering what was wrong with him.

In meetings with the public defender, she cried, unable to understand why she could not return home to her own bed.

Only after she had physically healed did she understand why she was imprisoned, the crash photos tormenting her sleep, with death her only release.

She attempted suicide many times using anything, even swallowing a sock, or a plastic fork, to bring relief.

Hope, for Lucia, was finding a way to die. She spent every moment with the thought and made other attempts. Lucia banged her head against the cell door and was medicated after rubbing the skin of her wrist against the wall, creating a burn that led to bleeding, but not infection.

In those first weeks, she hated herself and wished she could tear off her skin. The enormity of the tragedy was a constant companion that a prescribed antidepressant fashioned into a breathless ghost to sit beside her, to walk, eat, and sleep with her.

Despite the attempts of her female, Hispanic lawyer who tried sympathy, logic, pep talks from Jesus, or anger to make Lucia attend the trial, she refused and only appeared in court to plead guilty to two counts of vehicular manslaughter.

Lucia insisted on staying behind the walls of her cell, refusing visitors and was forced to eat and drink by interns in the medical ward.

It was during these early days when her father, raking grass on a blisteringly hot July day, died of a heart attack, his body found near the shade of a maple tree.

His coworkers had joked, "Wake up! It's not time for siesta."

At forty-nine, Jesus Martinez senior left the world—the father who Lucia could never disappoint, could never make angry or sad, the co-signer of her car loan.

Ten years later, Anna Martinez would ignore the pain in her side until pancreatic cancer ate her from the inside out and left her beyond hope. She, too, left the world-weary earth torn between the wonder of her beautiful grandchildren and the sadness of what might have been for her impish, clever daughter, who in eighth grade had died her hair with streaks of blond to be more "Anglo."

Over time, Lucia believed she was worthy of nothing, not the salvation offered by the prison prayer group, or the kindness of the white, chubby male psychologist who listened politely, sighed, then patted her softly on the shoulder when their sessions ended. She accepted her fate, her punishment, as the years passed. It was only right she suffer for the careless mistake and unimaginable tragedy she had befallen upon an unsuspecting grandmother and grandchild.

In those early prison years, her mind clouded by prescription drugs and minimal human interaction, she moved through the hazy hallways of the day-to-day, expressionless, lethargic and as empty as a crumpled bag. It was only when forced to "do something" as the psychologist had implored, did she sense the slightest ember of whom she had been. Learning to help others—the bandages, swabs, antiseptic and psychology of caring for patients—gradually softened the hardened scales of self-loathing.

And now in the van with her brother, she felt a glimmer of hope, the tiniest sense of her old self and of family.

8

On Saturday morning, Laura waited until the last minute to tell Jamella about her planned visit to the Arabian.

"We're going for a hike," she said, teasingly, unwilling to specify where.

"What? Why?" Jamella said, fidgeting with her shoelaces. "Are we going to see the horse?"

Laura placed two store bought cinnamon rolls into a brown paper bag but hid two carrots in her coat pocket.

"I hadn't planned on walking that way."

"Please, please! I won't say anything stupid."

"Or rude?"

"I won't say anything at all!" she said, opening the door.

"You might want to put a jacket on before going outside," Laura said.

Jamella climbed the embankment with long, hoppy strides, then waited at the crest for Laura.

"I should've had you carry these," Laura said, breathing deeply. "Here, take them."

Jamella grabbed the bag.

"This is what, another gift?"

"We're trying to make a friend, remember? Food helps."

They walked the hilly path leading to the open field and barn. The sun was warm and the air smelled of melting snow and wet earth. Near the back door of the house, purple crocus stood in overgrown clumps along the gravel walkway. The barn door was open, and Ace lay in the hay and sun by the entrance with his eyes closed. Their approach roused the old dog to stand upon its front legs.

Jamella stopped, placing her arm in front of her mother.

"What's wrong," Laura asked, but the girl didn't respond.

Instead, Jamella watched as Skip brushed Cal with long sweeps from the horse's neck down and across to its hind leg.

Laura instantly recognized Jamella's deep-eyed focus and waited, wondering what stirred in her artist's mind. The long, repetitive arcs of the soft brush against Cal's black coat fell before the girl like steps through a forested path leading to where shape and color become one.

With eyes closed, Jamella instinctively moved her left hand to trace light and form. After a few imaginary strokes, Jamella opened her eyes and smiled brightly.

"Looks like you figured something out," Laura said.

Instead of the traditional pencil drawings of the man standing with the horse, the girl would create sketches with faded edges. She would draw Cal in sweeps of black highlighted with the slightest of white streaks while the old man appeared as a silhouette of color and shape in deference to Cal, whose form was as striking a combination of darkness and light as one saw in the night sky.

Before the school year's end, Jamella would create many drawings of Cal, Ace, and Skip, sometimes together, sometimes alone, with Skip never fully realized or in sharp focus. Skip, his home, or barn were never central to her work, but included as background or grounding points for the horse standing or grazing in flowing poses of naturalness and grace.

Ace turned his head toward Skip, then woofed. The old man, spotting Laura and Jamella, shook his head. Jamella skipped over to him.

"What are you doing?" she asked.

"Good morning," Laura said. "We brought a couple of cinnamon buns to replace what Ace smooshed yesterday."

"They're day-olds from the store," Jamella said.

Skip stood, right hand bouncing against the side of his brown overalls.

"I spoke to John yesterday," Laura said. "He didn't think you'd mind."

Sliding his hand from the handle of the bristle comb, he said, "I do mind."

His eyes were like stone.

"And you're not here to visit. What *do* you want?"

"I want to be friends," Jamella said.

"Don't need any," Skip said.

He then led the horse by its mane to the field.

Laura froze, but Jamella followed him outside.

Skip patted Cal on his hind leg before closing the field gate. Jamella ducked between the fence rails and followed the horse with Ace trailing behind. The horse stopped at an exposed yellow-green patch of grass. Head down, it bit at the few shiny blades that rose to the sun.

Laura stopped Skip as he walked to the house.

"Would you please reconsider? I'll be with her," Laura asked. "She *loves* that horse."

Skip pointed a shaking finger at Laura.

"I don't want anyone here at night. You're the parent. You tell her *no*."

With hands on hips, Laura said, "She snuck out once! It won't happen—"

"No father, either," Skip said with a shake of his head, "to keep her in line."

"What? She's well behaved."

Skip smirked.

"Hope you know what you're doing adopting one of these—"

Like spitting, she said, "One of these *what?*"

Skip glared, lower jaw trembling, arm shaking by his side.

"Just stay off my damn property!"

Laura waved to Jamella, who held a crooked stick for Ace.

"Jamella!" she called.

The girl turned, eyes wide.

"Let's go. Now!"

Alarmed, the girl moved quickly, keeping pace with her mother.

Once together, Jamella asked, "What's wrong? Why are we going?"

"I'll tell you later."

"Aw—"

"Not now, please," Laura said, breathing heavily.

John, having finished vacuuming the living room rug, planned on a pot of coffee, but his father interrupted him.

Standing inside the back door, Skip said, "Why did you invite the woman and her kid? Looking for an owl? Right. That girl is looking to steal something."

John laughed.

"Steal what? Honestly, have you looked at this place, or yourself, lately? Your belt's about to rip apart, your shoes are worn, and this house," he said, raising his arms out wide, "is a dump."

"Ah, that's bull," Skip said, waving his hand at John. "You're always trying to be nice. Typical salesman, but that lady thinking she can save the world is a pipe dream."

John sat at the kitchen table, watching as Skip's eyes traced the wood grain pattern of the hardwood floor. The old man leaned against the sink, arms folded, drool slipping from the corner of his mouth.

John asked, "Is all this nonsense because the little girl's black?"

Skip's eyes widened, surprised by his son's ignorance of the world.

"Nonsense? For god sakes, they're running wild these days!"

"No, they're not."

"It's on the news every night—those Antifa riots, shootings, drugs," Skip said. "World's going to hell."

"Stop watching television," John said, surprised by Skip's conviction. "Never heard you talk like that before or be so angry."

"I'm wise to those two. Nothing but trouble."

Rather than argue, John asked, "When's the last time you saw a doctor?"

"For what?" Skip said. "Nothing wrong with me."

Skip reached for a glass in the cupboard by the sink.

"The tremor. It's worse."

Skip's hand shook as he held a cup under the cold water faucet.

"I manage," he said.

"Dad, make an appointment." John watched as water slipped from his father's lips and trickled over his bony Adam's apple like rain from a leaky gutter.

"Nah," Skip said, after finishing his drink. "Not interested in taking pills. That's all doctors do these days."

John, considering a reply, sensed the awkwardness of talking to a stranger.

"Whatever you think," John said. "But being rude to the neighbor isn't okay. If I'm here, they can visit, period. You won't have to be bothered."

"Oh, so you're the boss now? Never around, but now you're in charge?"

"Guess I showed up in time," he said with patience. "No reason to be mean to a little girl."

When Skip didn't reply, John said, "Nothing will be stolen. We know where they live. And, for sure, Ace and Cal are sick of looking at you."

The old man smirked.

"You're not much to look at either."

Later, John visited with Laura and said, "I'm sorry he spoke to you that way. He's gotten bitter."

They sat in a newly renovated kitchen, with dark blue quartz countertops, stainless steel appliances and white cabinets.

"He's not himself," John said, "or maybe I never saw that side of him. How's Jamella?"

"She's fine. I told her your dad had a headache," Laura said. "She went straight to her room to sketch the horse. But she'll be happy to visit once in a while."

"Probably more than that. There's a lot to do and he's not up to it. Let's exchange phone numbers," John said, "so you can bring your daughter."

My daughter, she thought, feeling validated, whole. *Yes, she is.*

Looking into the living room, he said of the drop cloths draped over the sofa and couch, "Doing some painting?"

Laura shook her head.

With a smile she said, "We tried, now I'm looking for someone to do a few rooms instead. Looked easier than it is."

He nodded, his eyes flat, without light, tired.

"Painting's not my thing, either."

As he stepped onto the back porch, Laura thanked him for thinking of Jamella, then said, "I owe you a favor. Let me do your tax returns, and your wife's, too."

John reflexively rubbed his wedding band. Carol's pointy cheeks shone in the angled porch light.

"Maybe just mine," he said, softly, taking the ring from his finger. "I'm divorced."

Reacting to her surprise, he added, "Probably shouldn't wear this, huh?"

The tall man took a step back, his eyes on Laura.

"Don't worry. I'm not stalking my ex or anything."

An unsettled air of anxiety or embarrassment, she was not sure which, or both, clung to him. An awkward, first date vibe simmered, but she dismissed it as silly, too hopeful. She felt an attraction, but wondered about him. Why wear the wedding ring? Was John a hopeless romantic with a broken heart, pathetically in denial, or weird?

"That's good to know," she said evenly. "How long?"

"Fifteen years. It's not about my ex, Carol. It's more of a keepsake. Tried it on the other hand, but," he shrugged, "feels like home on the left. Stupid, I know. Ever get that feeling of something being locked in, you know, just right?"

"I have," Laura said, the night air chilling her slipper-covered toes. "It's how I ended up with Jamella. Felt right."

"Of course." He stepped from the porch. "We'll be in touch. Good luck finding a painter."

They watched, Laura from the kitchen window and Jamella from the bedroom, as John navigated the hill, bent at the knees, hands out for balance.

Excited, Jamella called to Laura, "Did he say I could visit?"

"Maybe next weekend."

Jamella sat on the top step, disappointed.

"Maybe!"

"I think it's just for now," Laura said, grabbing the handrail. "His son is nice, and things might change."

"When?"

"After a good night's rest," she said, moving up the stairs. "Scoot. Time for bed."

Jamella struggled to sleep until an idea came to her. She would stand at the property line with the binoculars and watch Cal. It was not like being close to Cal, but it was the next best thing. Jamella closed her eyes, pleased with having devised a plan to make everyone happy, and maybe, too, the horse would come to her.

Jamella spent Monday and Tuesday standing by the edge of the property line on the side of the barn away from Skip's home. She would occasionally whistle, kick at the leaves, or throw small sticks to get the horse's attention.

After two days, and the horse barely acknowledging her, she decided to bring a carrot tied to a spool of kite string. On Wednesday, she scooched as close as she could to Skip's property line, swinging the carrot over her head like a lasso. When ready, she tossed it over the wood fencing and thirty feet into the field. This caught not only Cal's attention, who sniffed the air, but the old man's as well.

"Well, I'll be damned," he said, as he washed his hands at the kitchen sink.

Jamella heard Ace bark, the dog making excited circles around Skip as he walked slowly to her. She hurriedly pulled the carrot closer to her, disappointed that Cal no longer followed it. She quickly reeled in the twine, the carrot banging against the top rail and twirling upward like a majorette's baton. With her back turned to Skip, she put the carrot in a jacket pocket. Luckily, his uneven gait gave her time to pitch the reel down the embankment behind her.

"Hey! You! I see you there. What are you up to?"

Skip stopped ten feet from her, the gurgle of a wheeze in his chest.

"I'm just watching the horse," she said calmly. She then took a step back. "And I'm on my property, not yours."

"Oh, are you now?" Skip shook his head.

Without anger he said, "I'm too old for this."

"How old are you?"

"Old enough to know trouble when I see it. Now, get going! Don't want you around."

"I want to watch the horse, that's all."

He stared her, holding her gaze until she knew he wouldn't relent.

"Fine," she said, turning away.

Technically, she complied with Skip's request, standing back from the tree line for the next two days. She was tempted to tie two carrots together, but didn't want to miss her chance to see the horse on the weekend. Instead, she sat hidden under the trees, binoculars trained on the horse, watching how the light moved over Cal's muscles causing varying shades of bright black to a dark gray.

Watching the horse, she marveled at its easy gait and the cut of its muscles. Cal, too, had a tail that swung slowly like a clock pendulum, but with time seemingly stopped. Her fascination with the animal kept her hand moving over the scrap paper she had in her lap as minutes, then an hour, passed. Each arc of the pencil was scrutinized against the real thing until the light faded and she was called inside.

"How's the drawing coming?" Laura asked, glad the girl was amusing herself since Laura was busy during tax season.

"Good. I'm learning a lot about color and light."

"Really? That's great."

"Just wish I could be closer. Touch it. There's a special energy to it, but I'm not sure what it is."

"It's beautiful, for sure," Laura said, as Jamella set the dinner table. "It's the idea of the ideal. That means it's perfect. No trouble with John's dad?"

"No. He can't see me. Just wish he wasn't so hung up about the color of my skin."

Laura was about to raise an objection, but why? She was right.

"Let's hope he changes," Laura says.

"He'll die first," she said, grabbing forks from a drawer.

"Wouldn't surprise me, but let's be hopeful."

With a smile she added, "Like a miracle hopeful."

9

"Do you like it?" Jesus asked of the third-floor tenement apartment he had freshly painted for Lucia.

"Remember this?" he said, of her old bedroom set. "Thought your first night should feel like home."

"You kept this?" she said, running a hand over the shiny pine top of the dresser.

She opened the bottom drawer to find a small musical jewelry box, a gift from her grandmother when Lucia entered first grade. Inside was a plated gold necklace with a "Lucia" nameplate, and a pair of gold, oval shaped door-knocker earrings. Under the box sat two compact music discs by Jennifer Lopez and Ricky Martin. She was rocking to Martin's song, "Livin' la Vida Loca," on her car radio before the accident.

"I kept what I could," Jesus said, not wanting to mention donating her clothes, shoes, and jackets to charity years ago, but keeping the blue blanket bed covering which smelled faintly of cedar and a high school yearbook.

"The furniture is basic. Kept it simple. Wasn't sure what you'd like."

She sat on the bed.

Running her hand across the bed covering she said, "I don't know what to say."

Jesus had been good to her, done so much. She was overwhelmed with gratitude, but wasn't prepared to live on her own, pay bills, or find a job.

In prison, nothing but the repetitiveness of each day was real. Lucia's finding a job, being free, having a life of her own existed in thin, smoky dreams.

Now, with the cold walls, steel bars, and the mindless routine gone, the actuality of freedom was unreal, too much to process. She took deep breaths, then exhaled through rounded, dry lips.

"Easy, Little Sister," Jesus said, patting her shoulder. "Take a hot shower, watch some TV and get some sleep. I'll pick you up in the morning at eight. One step then another, okay?"

Lucia took his warm, dry hand and rested a cheek upon it. Like someone who had nearly drowned, she was relieved and exhausted.

"One step," she repeated, before releasing his hand.

Later, after a long, hot shower, she lay in bed listening to the footsteps and chatter of tenants when she realized she had not asked why Jesus would be along early in the morning. She was impressed with Maria and Roberto, who were polite and humble, barely smiling when Jesus spoke proudly of their good grades and "fútbol" skills. They were captains of their high school soccer teams, Maria earning the honor as a sophomore, while both had been varsity players since freshman year.

"We've played against each other since we were little," Roberto offered. "Maria's very good."

"Will you play next year in college?" Lucia asked.

"Hope so," he said, of the community college team.

Later, when she and Jesus were alone Lucia said, "You've done well. Businessman, property owner, parent—those two are special."

Jesus nodded.

"All thanks to their mother. Good woman. I was loco then."

"And now?" Lucia said, teasingly, remembering the young women he chased with bright eyes and an easy cool. *"Tienes muchas navias?"*

Jesus laughed.

Waving his hand across his face he said, "Ya no. Not a lot of girlfriends. Work is all. The business keeps me busy."

Jesus's smile lingered in her mind as she drifted off to sleep on a soft, warm mattress.

After a week of watching the horse and dealing with its grumpy owner, Jamella decided to do some internet research about their crusty neighbor. She was flustered that John had not called, and decided she had to find a way to get the old man to change his mind. What she found stunned her.

Jamella woke to the Sunday morning's first light and went to Laura.

"Get up, please," she said, tapping upon her mother's shoulder. "I know something really sad."

Laura rubbed her eyes.

"This *better* be good," she said. "It's way too early."

Jamella placed the laptop on the bed.

"Look, his wife and granddaughter died."

"Who?" Laura said, sliding up against the headboard.

Squinting against the screen's glare, she read a local newspaper article, "Local Woman and Child Killed in DUI Crash."

Jamella stood by the window, eyes focused on the entrance to Skip's driveway and littered cans on the lawn.

"How sad," Laura said softly.

"Why would someone do that?" Jamella asked.

"I don't think anyone planned to do it," Laura said, feeling the cold gust of an opened door into John's world.

"They did it on purpose," Jamella said of the pile of trash, her eyes shining with anger. "Look at all the garbage. It's so mean!"

The girl stomped out of the room, grabbed a coat and then slipped on the sneakers left by the door. With a black trash bag in hand, she walked out before Laura could ask her to stop.

Rather than follow, Laura went to the window and watched Jamella, arms swinging with purpose, walk the road to Skip's, in her blue and white striped flannel pajama pants. Laura pulled the collar of her robe tighter to her neck and shivered. The furnace rumbled awake as she curled into a soft chair, eyes on her daughter.

Jamella grabbed cans, cardboard beer containers and plastic "nip" bottles and dropped them into the trash bag, which curled in the wind like a dog twisting against its leash.

Laura was no match for Jamella's energy most days, but today Laura was empty, exhausted, the news of the car wreck taking her strength and clouding her thoughts. So sad, was all she could think.

Jamella was unaware of Skip, who had not so quietly approached her, even calling to her as he walked.

"What's all this about?" he said, causing Jamella to stop.

Ace shuffled to her and sniffed. Sitting at the girl's feet, the dog turned its head toward Skip.

"Picking up trash won't change my mind."

Jamella rolled her eyes.

"Don't want to. Can't change your mind anyway."

"That's right," he said confidently.

"You only like white people."

Skip scoffed.

"What would you know about that? You're a little—"
Ace barked.

"See?" Jamella said. "Even a dog can tell. Lots of white people just act nice."

"Or maybe, Smarty Pants, it's better to stick to our own," he said, thinking of his time in Vietnam and the black and white soldiers under his command.

"Better for what?" she asked, dumping beer from a can onto the grass.

"Bah," he said, waving his hand at her. "You're too young to know anything," he said, dismissively. "It makes life easier for everybody, that's what."

She stood straight and looked into Skip's eyes.

"Weird. You have a black horse and dog, but that's okay."

"That's not the same," Skip said, feeling superior. "With people, it's always been that way."

In Vietnam, the white men in his platoon had cheered the murder of Martin Luther King by waving the Confederate Navy Jack, infuriating black soldiers. Malcolm X, the Nation of Islam, and King were all hell-raisers and a pain in the army's backside. With King gone, the focus would be on the enemy, he assumed, and not on each other, but there was no harmony. Fights broke out in service clubs, and Skip was glad to leave for home in sixty-eight. The disharmony and near chaos unseated his sense of rule and order and preemptively ended his military career.

"I'm eleven," she said. "I don't know how it's been, but if it's not good, it's not good."

"Just like that, huh?" He wanted to add, life isn't so simple, but didn't.

"Yup. Like this," she said, waving arms above the litter, "makes me mad."

She jabbed at the trash, punching it into the black bag until the plastic bulged and stretched with beer cans, fast food Styrofoam, and stiff cardboard.

"People can be *so* mean."

The truth silenced him. He expected her to stop, but she kept working with Ace moving beside her.

Skip stood silently, head bowed, the roadway quiet, air whooshing through the nearby pines. The cold breeze slapped at the old man's cheeks. *She's right. Either it's right or wrong, it* is *that simple.*

The black men in his platoon had expected Skip to temper the celebratory hate directed at them, but he declined, knowing it was better to lose some soldiers' respect than all.

"Look," he had said to Benny, a black soldier, parroting the advice of his superiors, "I appreciate how you want this to stop, but I can't undo two hundred years of history."

But he had failed them. Skip followed the advice of his superior, which was to stay out of it.

"If we side with them, all hell will break loose. You wouldn't be the first lieutenant in the battle zone to take a bullet in the back. That's what we're up against."

Skip could have bucked his commanding officer, asked his men to refocus, but he took the easy way out. Skip had planned on the military as a career, and advocating for his black soldiers would make him a malcontent.

Instead, brave men who had saluted him, respected him, and did all he had asked would later barely look him in the eye, including Benny, who had approached Skip on behalf of the others. So much for courage on the battlefield, Skip mused after he was stateside, when he could not muster anyone in support of his black soldiers.

Ultimately, he resolved they had expected too much in the moment, but it never left him. The disappointment and resentment in his men's eyes was an unresolved consequence of his service, his lack of leadership. So be it, he thought, while moving on with life.

Jamella's determination to right a wrong, though, rekindled the past, his failure.

Watching her, the old man's mind fluttered though images and feelings kept in a quiet place until it settled, lightly and surprisingly, upon Libby. She liked to help and have little jobs. They had been a team. The urge to fix something stirred within him. Undone by Jamella's honesty and determination, Frank went to one knee, grabbed an empty plastic vodka bottle and handed it to Jamella.

"We can be mean without trying," he said, eye to eye with the girl.

Jamella paused.

"Why?"

Taking the garbage bag from her hands, he said, "It's easy to do."

"Like mean kids," the girl said, nodding. "They don't care either."

With her eyes on his, Jamella added, "I read about what happened a long time ago. The car accident. That was sad."

Skip stood, his face turned to the side. Jamella's small act of kindness was complete in its upheaval of all things kept barely secured in the past.

"Can't ever get away from it," he muttered.

"Get away from what?"

"The past," he said, with a sigh. "You read it somewhere?"

"Yes, look, I'm sorry!" she said, feeling something was wrong.

He shook his head.

"Had to be on the computer. Got every damn thing on it."

The girl stood, hands clenched into fists.

"I won't say it again. I promise," she said, waiting and hoping to please him.

He nodded.

One foot placed in front of the other had led to now, to standing with a mixed-race child who had so simply spotted the veiled hate on his soul as she might a favorite candy mixed with others in a bowl.

Jamella was an odd kid, he would say later to John. "That girl's got spunk. Speaks her mind."

Before she turned to leave, he said, "You're right about me. Come over in the afternoon."

"Okay," she said, eyes wide. "I will!"

Later that morning, as he stood in church during Mass, Skip asked God for forgiveness. He would not confess his sin against Jamella to the priest, though. Clergymen today were not like those of the past, who understood how different folks kept to themselves and nobody complained. No, God was a witness to his failure, his sins of cowardice and hate.

Confessing, though, was not for Skip who considered priests to be like captains or platoon leaders. Some were good, some were bad, and he would rather take his orders directly from the Lord. He knew kindness was required, and he asked once again, as he had many times, for God to bless the men he had failed.

As the Mass continued, Jamella's no nonsense way of speaking brought a smile to his lips. She knew what she wanted, was unafraid to act, and had grit. What would be the harm in letting her visit the horse? At that, a warmth filled his heart in ways he had not felt in years.

A voice from behind whispered, "Skip," and he realized the parishioners were now seated, so he sat, thinking of Jamella and his next steps.

10

ucia woke at dawn unsure of what to do first so she did nothing. Instead, she lay watching the sky outside the window brighten from gray to pink to blue. Many times, she had imagined her first week of freedom, but she never thought past one day—a visit to her brother and then, what? Shopping, meeting old friends or taking a walk on the beach was as far as her mind would take her.

In prison, lights on signified the beginning, and lights out was the end. With the sameness of each day, the connections to friends, family, and the uniqueness of one's self, disappeared. She could not remember what her favorite hand cream smelled like, or how smooth leather felt. She wore, ate, and drank what was issued. Lucia made no decisions, planned nothing, and moved through the day from one station—eat, work, study, free time—to the next.

Now she lay warm, quiet, unhurried, and overwhelmed with relief. Her first step removed from a past life. Another hot shower would be wonderful tonight, she thought, as she rose to dress and wait for Jesus.

On the floor by the bathroom vanity sat a gift bag of toiletries which held a makeup kit, deodorant, hairbrush, soap and lip gloss from Maria and Roberto. Towels, face cloths, bubble bath, and laundry detergent stood on the bath closet shelves. When Lucia had thanked Jesus, he joked the items were left behind by the prior tenant.

"All of them unopened, like new!" Lucia said, feigning surprise. "Oh. How lucky for me."

Standing before the mirror, she applied lip gloss and sadly noted the wrinkles around her eyes and mouth. She would consider makeup later.

When she was a toddler, her father would tease, "Your eyes, my *Chiquita*, are Oreos floating in milk. I'm going to eat them!"

She smiled thinking of the chase before the kisses of his soft beard on her cheeks.

Lucia was waiting by the front hallway door of the building when Jesus arrived.

"Here's the plan," Jesus said, driving the work van from the curb, "price two jobs, then we stop at the market. *Como es que?*"

"That's fine," Lucia said.

"First stop is breakfast," he said, turning into a parking lot three blocks from Lucia's apartment. "This bodega is why I bought the building that you're in. *Molletes* are very good. Later, you can see my place."

"What about the old neighborhood?" she said, as they stood in line at the deli counter.

She ordered a *mollete* with black beans and cheese.

They ate the breakfast sandwiches in the front seat of the van.

"Mm," Lucia said, "so good."

She stopped herself from saying, "Haven't had one of these in a long time", because everything was new. She would think it though, many times over the days and weeks ahead.

"The old neighborhood has changed. You'll see," Jesus said, crumpling the paper sandwich wrapper.

"Good or bad?"

"Remember I told you the colleges had opened extensions along the river?" he said, turning the ignition key. "Well, new money came in."

They were driving on the street now, the van's suspension squeaking with each bump, traveling toward their childhood home.

"What I didn't tell you was that I sold our home for this," he said, rubbing the tips of fingers on his right hand together, "Mucho dinero. *Crazy* money. I held out for a long time, but the neighborhood was changing fast, so why not? Very Anglo now, you'll see."

At the intersection, two, four story brick buildings stood, dwarfing the River Street sign secured to a steel lamppost. Jesus parked the van across from a busy coffee shop.

"Wait, what?" Lucia said. "That's our house?"

The front porch extended to the street and the picture window was now an "order here" take-out. Customers sipped coffee and nibbled pastries while seated at small round, wrought iron tables in what was once a double parlor. The hardwood floor and half wainscoted walls had the same shiny veneer she remembered. The three back bedrooms were gone, opening the space with only the original kitchen and bathroom remaining.

"Want to check it out?" Jesus asked.

She nodded, eyes scanning the multi-tiered vehicle garages and the long grass park snaking along by the river, having replaced the homes of childhood friends and families. Further along, the tenement homes of her youth remained, but no children rode bikes or skipped rope.

"The park and the river . . . wow," Lucia said, of the sun flashing off the gently flowing blue water. "So clean. Is the apartment above the coffee shop rented, too?" she asked, thinking of her mother's sister, Aunt Lucy, who made *Turrón de Navidad*—honey and almond nougats—at Christmas. Lucy had cared for Anna when the woman's cancer made her helpless. Unmarried, the aunt had lived alone since Jesus and Lucia could remember. While no one spoke of it, Lucy was a closeted lesbian who kept an underground social life. Still, she died alone.

"Yes. Every inch is profitable. Very smart," Jesus said. "When Lucy passed, I sold. Glad they didn't tear it down. A little something of us is still here. Remember the cement we put our initials in?"

Lucia smiled.

"We should've used a stick instead of our fingers. Took forever to chip off."

"So, let's talk money," he said, as he drove the van from the curb.

"Money?" she said, sad but impressed by the neighborhood transformation.

"From the house. We have three properties. One I own outright and the one you live in is yours—"

"I live in?"

Jesus nodded.

White, college aged men and women crossed the street at the red light, shoulders hunched against the chilling wind off the river.

"I put both our names on the deed, so it's yours to do what you want. The third one is a rental. That money goes into a joint savings account with our names on it, too. We're partners. It's right around the corner from the one you own. Now, if the hospital expands—"

"Wait," Lucia said, eyes squinted. "How could you sign papers when I was inside?"

Jesus winked.

"Asked a lady friend."

He pulled his index finger and thumb together.

"Just a *mentira piadosa*—a little one—to help us out. I had to plan for you."

A white lie, she thought, noting the occasional black or brown faces, mostly wearing college issued maintenance overalls, walking the street.

"So, you bought me a house?"

"Ah, no—*mamá y papá*—our inheritance."

"It's too much," she said, eyes welling with tears.

"No, the money part is good," he said, but she didn't reply.

Instead, with hands to her face, a deep sob rose from her chest. Too much too soon, he knew.

They rode out of the city in silence, Lucia weakened by gratitude and loss. Her parents, hard workers, had left behind what they owned, their legacy, and Jesus had multiplied it. The good brother who had looked out for a silly girl, his *manita*, Lucia, who'd barely finished high school, more interested in sharp-looking clothes, makeup, flirty boys, and chatty friends than books. Jesus went from chasing girls to saving money, and his industriousness shamed her. Charming Jesus, who always had pretty girls on his arms and something exciting to do, had planned for Lucia's life after prison without being asked. Her cheeks reddened with anger. Pride stung, she was determined to be an asset to him, to repay him in all the ways someone who is loyal and thoughtful deserved. As he parked the van in a driveway off the main road, she touched his arm.

"Whatever you need," she said, "I will do."

He smiled.

"Sure, but first we have to price a job. It's easy, you'll see."

11

"I can see Cal today!" Jamella said, as she slammed the front door closed.

"That's good news," Laura said as she patted the couch cushion, inviting Jamella to sit.

"Your good deed paid off, huh?"

"Yup," she said, snuggling to Laura and pulling a blue and white quilt to her chin.

"We talked about the accident, too."

"You did?" Laura said, louder than she intended. "And?"

Jamella, smoothing the wrinkles from the quilt with her left hand said, "He swore, 'Damn', about the internet. He doesn't like that."

"That's all?" Laura asked, Jamella's cold knees pressed against her legs.

"He doesn't like black people, either."

Laura tossed the quilt from her legs.

Standing, she said, "I can't believe he'd tell you that! I don't think you should be around him."

"Mom," Jamella said, laying sideways on the couch, "he didn't have to tell the truth. Plus, I think he kind of likes me."

Laura paused. *Why would he say that?* A simple, "Get lost, kid," would've been enough.

"And he said you can visit the horse?"

Jamella shivered under the quilt.

"Yeah, he was nice. It's freezing in here! Is the furnace broken?"

Laura, sitting upon the edge of the couch, placed her palm to Jamella's cool cheek.

"How did you feel when he said he didn't like black people?"

Jamella rolled her eyes.

"Mom, everybody around here is white. It happens all the time."

"Where? In school?"

"Everywhere. Don't you see them staring at us?"

Laura sighed.

"I didn't think you noticed. It happens at school, too?"

"And the bus," Jamella corrected. "School's okay, mostly."

Sitting up, she said, "I'm hungry."

Mother and daughter moved to the kitchen. Over scrambled eggs and cinnamon toast, Laura pressed Jamella, who spoke of the older boys who would say, "Hello, poop stain," if they passed her in the hall. Or, "I didn't know this bus goes to Africa."

"How awful," Laura said, slapping down on the table. "And they're only in the sixth grade! Have you told an adult?"

Jamella shook her head no.

"Well, I'm going to put a stop to that. If those boys think—"

"Mom," Jamella said, tapping a spoon against the side of a mug, "it's like Mister Skip said, 'It's the way it's always been,' that's why people stare. Plus, I'm an only. We're onlies."

"Like the only ones?" Laura said, reaching to take the spoon from the girl's hand.

Jamella rose.

"Most kids are nice, and Hannah tells them to drop dead."

A tight smile came to the girl's lips, knowing it was wrong to say, but it pleased Jamella.

"The boys are afraid of her because she's really pretty, and she has an older brother. She wants to be a lawyer, so she sticks up for me."

Laura smiled.

"I still think I should call the school."

Before Jamella could protest, the doorbell rang.

"Oh," Laura said, realizing she was still in her nightgown, "It's the painters. Can you let them in? I need to change."

Laura pulled on a white sweatshirt and blue jeans, then ran a brush through her hair while Jesus and Lucia waited with Jamella at the bottom of the stairs by the front door.

"They're nice," Jamella said, by way of introduction.

"But can they paint walls?" Laura said, smiling.

"I'm Jesus, and this is my sister—"

"Gloria," Lucia said, extending her hand. "My brother does good work."

Gloria, her middle name, felt right and strong in the moment.

"A new me," she would say later to Jesus on the ride to the market.

"I'm sure," Laura said. "Let me show you what we need."

They walked from room to room.

"Ceilings, too," Laura said, as they stepped into Jamella's room.

"Very, nice," Gloria said, of Jamella's pencil sketches laying on her bed and desk. "May I?"

Gloria sat with Jamella while Jesus and Laura went on to other rooms.

"I'm sure you know these are amazing," Gloria said, as she held them up to the window light.

"This one," she said of a blurred-eyed Skip, "is unfinished?"

Jamella nodded.

"I couldn't get it right, but I can now."

"How do you decide what to draw?"

"When something shines in here," she said, pointing to her temple, "I try to catch it, and it has to be just right, or I don't like it."

Gloria smiled at the intensity in Jamella's eyes.

"You should be proud. Now, I have to find my brother."

"Your skin is like mine," she said. "I hope you come back."

Gloria rose and turned to Jamella.

"I will," she assured her, not knowing if she ever would, but sensing Jamella's need.

"So, how long before you can start?" Laura asked, as she and Jesus stood in the kitchen.

"At least three weeks," Jesus said.

"I'll call," he said, reaching for the door. "Thank you."

By day's end, Jesus would bid and secure two more jobs, one of which was a drugstore ceiling to be done overnight.

Lucia learned how to measure for square feet and determine the type and amount of paint. She also added the cost of the materials to calculate a total price.

"Plenty of work to keep us busy, huh?" Jesus said at the end of the day, standing in Lucia's kitchen. "Tomorrow we get a phone for you, and heavy duty coveralls. Put it on the business account."

Lucia yawned as she placed a box of cereal in the cupboard.

Jesus placed a hand on her shoulder.

"It was a lot for a first day," he said. "One last thing, your cousins."

Lucia nodded.

"In time," she said, so many thoughts of the day arching like electrical wires.

"Sure, low key for now."

12

Jamella was inside the barn with Skip before Laura, who had trailed behind, scaled the hill.

"Thanks for waiting," she said to John, her face colored by exertion. "This never gets easy, does it?"

John smiled.

"Good for the heart, but that's about it. So, this is a surprise, huh? How'd you get him to change his mind?"

"It wasn't me," she said, walking along the fence.

Skip and Jamella were standing by Cal.

"That's it, real calm," Skip said, as the girl gently stroked Cal's back leg. "That's how you clean the hooves."

John whispered to Laura, "This is too good to be true."

He motioned to her to walk with him.

Outside, he said, "I spoke yesterday with his primary care doctor. Dad's been avoiding him. I made an appointment with a neurologist, too. Going to be a struggle to get him there."

"He seems okay," she said, watching as he scooped clods of dirt from Cal's rear hoof. "Attitude-wise, at least."

"I'm glad. I was disappointed in how he acted."

Skip ran his hand gently along Cal's leg, explaining to Jamella how to raise its hoof, when he stumbled forward onto his hands and knees.

Jamella dropped down to him, but he said, "No, no. Stay with Cal."

John hurried in.

"Are you okay?"

He grabbed Skip's arm.

"I'm fine," he said, stubbornly pulling it away.

Like a wooden folding ladder, he stiffly—one foot, then another—rose to his full height. He squeezed his eyes shut, hoping to force the dizzy fog from his head.

John, brushing sprigs of hay from Skip's pant legs asked, "Did you eat lunch?"

"Not yet," he said, reaching to pat Cal on the hind leg.

"Let's finish that last hoof," he said to Jamella.

"You try," he said, handing the hoof pick to her. "Careful."

Laura froze, not sure if it was wise to have her daughter bent over beside the horse. Cal stood passively, but Laura feared even the slightest kick was dangerous.

Jamella gently raised the horse's foot and slowly dug the tool into the frog of the foot, the triangled sole between its toes. She flicked a clod of mud from it, and later used a stiff brush to clean the remaining dirt. The horse never moved.

"Fast learner," Skip said. "Good. Let's get him to the field."

Jamella, eyes wide, face flushed with pride, walked with the old man and the horse out of the barn and into the bright afternoon sun.

"Whew," Laura said, thinking of how close Jamella's face had been to the horse's hoof, "that was a bit intense."

"Yes," John said, watching Skip standing by the fence. "He's got me worried."

Laura laughed.

"Looks like we're thinking two different things."

John turned and noticed the light from the field flicker in Laura's eyes.

"How's that?"

"I was afraid Cal would kick her."

"Nothing to worry about," John said with a shake of his head. "Cal's always been calm for an Arabian. Not high strung at all. My Elizabeth—Libby—learned how to ride her. See that pole over by the gate? Looks like an old clothesline hanging there? That's a trainer for horse riding," he paused, eyes fixed on the rusted pole tipped slightly to one side. "Libby started on that when she was six."

Laura, with her hand on John's forearm said, "I'm so sorry for your loss."

The warmth of her touch and kindness of Laura's words brought a long held sadness to his eyes. He blinked at a tear.

"She's in good hands."

Laura, unsure if he meant Libby or Jamella, waited.

"My dad's been around horses all his life," he said. "She'll be fine."

He placed his hand atop Laura's, mouth opened as if to continue but didn't. He let go of her hand and stepped toward the light of the open door.

"Thanks. The accident was a long time ago, but sometimes it seems," John's voiced trailed off and he sighed.

Forcing a smile, he offered his arm to her.

Laura hooked a hand to his elbow, and he sighed like someone taking a determined step forward.

Watching as Jamella stood on the bottom fence rail next to Skip, she said, "Looks like you'll be seeing a lot more of my daughter. Once she sets her mind on something, she's hard to shake."

"Like my dad," he said, as they walked. "Did you find a painter?"

"I just contracted with someone today. Why?"

"Have you seen the inside of this house?"

Before entering the kitchen, Laura paused. Skip, Jamella and Ace were by the fence, watching Cal, whose tail swayed from side to side.

"Idyllic," she said softly, before following John inside.

"I assume you're a tea drinker," he said. "Picked up a variety pack at the market today."

"I am," she said, "but a glass of water's fine. Don't want to stay too long. Are those walls pink?"

John smiled.

"Of course. Aren't all living rooms pink? See what I'm up against? It's been that color since I was a kid."

As he sipped water, she said, "You've got plenty to do."

"Yes," he said, placing the glass down onto the table. "And that's just the house. He's going to be a handful, too. He's stubborn and won't listen to his doctor who thinks he might have something serious going on with the tremor. And based on today, balance is a problem, too."

"Too bad doctors don't make house calls anymore," Laura said, absentmindedly counting the tiny roosters of the tablecloth print. "Classic role reversal, too. The child becomes the parent."

Instantly, Laura realized the potential error of referring to John as not having Libby, so she added, "I mean, you know, you and your dad."

John leaned forward, chin on hands, elbows on table. "How is it being a single mom?"

"Pretty easy when she's in school. Summertime's a challenge. She doesn't make friends easily."

The teakettle whistled, so she waited until it was off the burner.

"I've wondered lately if I made a mistake. She says we have no friends. We're onlies—her definition—meaning alone, but it's more pronounced for her. I hadn't thought of what it would be like for her in my world."

John agreed.

"A white one. Must feel lonely sometimes."

John's thoughts flashed to empty hotel rooms and the four-bedroom home they sat in, once so full of life.

"No foster home or old school friends?"

"No, none that she wants to see. Not sure why."

"Maybe," he said with mischief in his eyes, "she likes her friends much older...like in their seventies."

Laura rose from the table.

"If I'd only known," she said, smiling.

Turning to the back window, she said, "I never thought her being here would've happened, but I'm glad. She was infatuated with the horse."

"It's worked for both of them," John said, moving to the sink. "Dad was alone which made him grumpy."

"Lost his connection to people," Laura said, knowing how easy that could be.

Later, as Jamella and Laura waved goodbye, a flicker of life twirled in Skip's cold eyes.

"Nice to have visitors," John said, feeling relaxed.

Lucia's new cell phone buzzed with the few family contacts Jesus shared with her as they sat in the van in the mall parking lot.

"Maybe text our cousins first. Tell them you'll be in touch."

They spent the morning in a medical building hallway painting doorframes. Lucia enjoyed the work. Time passed with her mind focused on the smooth lines of paint made with the brush. Workers at the jobsite paid little or no attention to her as she did them. Once, she would have made eye contact with any man who walked past, but now she ignored them. She knew what she liked, a kind smile and bright, cheerful eyes. Luckily, she sorted faces quickly. She'd had both male and female guards and realized happy people were attractive and gave her hope.

Lucia's incarceration was spent listening more than talking and thinking of how everyone acted and why. Each day was another page in the larger story of how we become, how we live and what we think, want, or value. She developed a sense for how bodies moved and spoke in proximity to others, which at first she found interesting and fun.

Later, she would find it upsetting and intimidating to be able to predict conflict or watch hate flame from the slightest, imperceptible spark. The more she understood about others, the more she gravitated toward the few who smiled, who cared, or brought more than just what was minimally required or needed.

Lucia kept to herself, became wary of others, and avoided attention. She saved her best self for those whose hearts were true. She wondered often if she would have learned this lesson on the outside. After all, she was a silly girl then.

"Who wasn't?" Tina, one of the female nurse instructors replied offhandedly.

Lucia found Tina to be exceedingly attractive.

Tina Gomez was in her mid-forties and taught basic medical practices to aspiring inmates. She was married with two girls, wore no makeup, was round in hips and stomach, and looked tired often. She was so respected that she could run the whole prison without a guard if need be. She was brown-skinned, too, unlike other teachers.

Mrs. Gomez stood out because she cared beyond all measure, beyond more than she was paid to or her students deserved. Her endless well of empathy swelled Lucia's heart. Its nest of warmth and comfort made Lucia feel an intense love for someone beyond a family member or a girlish crush. Lucia's feelings for Tina were so strong she wondered about her own sexuality. Could she be physically in love with her?

In her private, intimate moments, though, Lucia realized it wasn't sexual, but powerful. Mrs. Gomez's unconditional, uncompromising care for the inmates in class allowed them to learn many things, the most important being dignity. The teacher's mantra was, "Empathy given is hope. Empathy shared is empowerment. And empathy accepted is obligation."

Those in Mrs. Gomez's orbit were fully realized human beings, even when they didn't know it. Tina's aptitude for kindness, for forgiveness of mistakes, and the gentle acceptance of human flaws brought Lucia comfort and allowed her to forgive, but not forget, her fatal mistake.

Lucia cried when Mrs. Gomez moved on to a better career opportunity and spoke of her at a last parole hearing.

"I didn't even notice Mrs. Gomez the first time she came into the classroom. I thought she was a janitor. She helped me realize there was always good to be done, and that I was always capable of better, no matter what."

Lucia paused, feeling exposed and sounding silly in the moment with infatuation, but realizing vulnerability is the courage of love.

In time, Lucia would no longer study others. Especially bothersome to her were those inmates who were selfish. They were the worst of the lot with their cunning, desperation, and cruelty. She avoided them, but she practiced kindness in preparation for her release, and spent the last years of prison as happy as one could be behind bars.

"Hey, Little Sister, what planet are you on?" Jesus asked, while in the driver's seat of the van. "You're zoning somewhere."

Lucia's eyes were on the phone in her hand.

"Sorry," she said. "I was thinking of a teacher I had in prison. Maybe someday I can call her."

"Sure, there are lots of things you can do now. My friend, Eddie—remember him? Wants to text you."

"Isn't he married?" she asked, as she opened and closed the apps on her cell phone.

"No, not for a long while. He was deployed three times. Guess it was too much."

Jesus drove to a housing development construction site.

"Big job for us here. Entire first and second floor, twenty units to do, ceilings, walls, and hallways."

Men in hard hats pointed and talked as they poured a cement patio near the entrance while others installed curbs for individual vehicle parking.

Inside, they walked the long, cinder block hallway and went to the first two-bedroom unit needing paint. The walls were bare and smelled of plaster.

"We're doing this whole building alone?"

"No. I have some guys coming Monday. I hire them as I need them."

Lucia helped Jesus carry five-gallon buckets of flat white paint, plastic sheeting, and painter's tape into different apartments.

After they had taken the last of the paint from the van, Jesus asked, "So Eddie. He's a good guy, you know. Just wants to talk. Asked if you were still pretty."

"And you told him, what?" she said, rubbing the callus on her right palm.

Grinning, he said, "Well, I couldn't lie."

Lucia laughed.

"Poor Eddie," she said.

13

Jamella proved to be a fast learner. So much so that Skip came to rely on her daily to feed and groom Cal. After dinner, she'd phone Skip, and he would meet her in the barn. She would add fresh water to a galvanized steel trough, put two bundles of hay in the holder hanging from the wall, and fill a pail with feed. She had earned the trust of the old man who, in turn, had to prove himself to Laura.

Laura and Skip had first agreed on Wednesday visits, where Jamella learned to care for the horse, assuming her schoolwork and reports were good.

Skip wore the same jeans and a threadbare, worn-at-the-sleeves flannel jacket. He was not much for polite conversation. Instead, he was practical and concerned with the weather or interested in reports on Jamella's behavior and academics.

Laura worried about leaving Jamella with Skip. She considered him a cranky bigot and wondered about his impact on Jamella, but Skip's influence was positive. Laura found that her daughter focused more in class and used binders—a habit of Hannah's—to keep lessons organized. By March, she let Jamella go to the barn unaccompanied, wearing a reflective vest and carrying a flashlight and a Tracfone. She did pop in on occasion to see how things were going.

While dishes drip-dried in the sink, Laura walked the highway and then Skip's driveway, enjoying the damp earth smell with the change of winter to spring. She quietly approached the barn, intent on listening and watched as Jamella brushed Cal, her right hand on the horse and the left moving in gentle, caressing arcs. Skip sat on a bale of hay, beer in hand, dog resting at his feet. Neither spoke, although Jamella would coo softly, reassuring the horse. Laura wondered about Skip's change of heart, as Jamella wasn't easy to warm up to. Then again, neither was the old man. They were linked by straight-line mindsets and the love of a horse.

Having grown up without pets, Laura was surprised by the change in Jamella. She was calmer and more purposeful with the horse as her responsibility. She caressed Cal as much as she groomed it. Slowly, gently, her cheek against the horse's side, listening to its heart beat. Skip sat, smiling slightly, his eyes glazed over in thought. He was thinner now than he was a month ago, his head and neck sunk into the collar of his jacket. She would ask John on Saturday about his father's appetite. For now, though, Laura stood out of sight, enjoying the satisfaction a parent holds for a happy child.

Skip rose, calling, "Okay, Miss J, time to go."

Jamella returned the brush to a rack by the corral.

"Another fine day's work. Cal's never had it so good."

Jamella nodded, her face flushed with pride.

"Is it okay if Hannah comes on Saturday?"

As they stepped from the barn, Laura said, "Hello. Looks like I'm just in time. Thanks again," she said to Skip, his face pale.

He okayed the girl's request.

"Good, you'll like her," Jamella said. "She's quieter than me."

They walked the driveway, Jamella skipping side to side. Jamella said Skip was interested in her math lessons.

"He was an engineer or something like that. He talked about drawings with numbers and stuff."

"Does he talk much about his work?"

"No, that's all. He's quiet. Sometimes he mumbles, but I don't know what it means."

"You don't ask?"

"It's private."

"Good thinking."

Jamella instinctively moved closer to her mother once they stepped onto the main road. Engine noise and flying sand from fast moving cars upset Jamella, who walked with hands over her ears.

"I want to put a stop littering sign here," she said, pointing to Skip's front yard. "People ignore the one on the pole."

"There's lots of trash all along here," Laura said. "We should do something tomorrow."

By noon on Saturday, they had filled three trash bags within the thirty yards between their driveway and Skip's.

"That was a nasty job," Laura said, holding Jamella's sign, "Please don't litter!" as the girl drove bamboo tomato stakes into the roadside.

"It's windy," Laura said to Jamella, whose fingers twisted the twine, "be sure it's tight."

John stopped his car in Skip's driveway.

"Two signs, huh?" he called through the open passenger side window, "should do the trick. Didn't know you did highway maintenance, too."

Laura smiled.

"No, just a good deed."

"I've got lunch," he said, of the two warm pizza boxes on the front seat. "Hop in."

Skip sat in the living room, clean laundry in a basket at his feet and an unfolded towel in his lap, asleep.

"Rough night, Dad?" John asked.

The old man awoke to Jamella standing by him.

"I can help," she said, taking the towel from his lap.

"Let's eat first," John said, carrying dishes to the dining room table.

Jamella set out napkins while Laura opened the pizza boxes. Skip was the last to sit at the head of the table, watching, his hand twitching atop the back of the chair.

"Dad?" John said, of the plate of warm pizza placed on the table in front of the old man.

Skip sat. Tipping his head closer to the table, he shakily slid the tip of the slice through his lips. Ace placed his jaw upon the old man's leg, hoping for a bite. Skip chewed slowly, listening to how Laura and Jamella spent the morning by the road.

At last, he said, "Thank you," and instantly coughed hoarsely, his face contorted and demon red.

Ace barked, while John jumped to Skip's side.

"He does that a lot," Jamella said, between bites. "Wrong pipe."

John nodded, his eyes wide with concern.

Skip coughed again, but the color in his face drained and his breathing slowed. He sipped some soda, as tears slipped from his eyes. With a deep breath, he cleared his throat.

"He's better now," Jamella said.

"Not liking this, Dad," John said. "Glad you have an appointment this week. I'm going with you. I want to hear what the doc has to say."

"Ah," Skip said, barely above a whisper, "I'm fine."

After Jamella cleared the table, she accompanied Skip out to the field. The horse, out by the far side of the fence, broke into a fast walk, hooves thumping. With each step, lean muscle from shoulder to knee flexed and shone in the afternoon light. Its mane bounced gently while the tail hopped and swayed.

To Jamella's eyes, Cal split the air like a canoe through calm water. She knew black, the shade of shadow, night, fear, apprehension and knew it was why she was stared at and teased. Cal was different, though. The horse changed how Jamella saw black. Cal was graceful, powerful, calm, and gentle. Color depended upon how it was used to be real, effective, eye-catching, and memorable. Being with Cal let her skin belong to her, let it be special. A smile came to her face.

Skip said, "Looks like you're happy to see each other."

Jamella stood on the bottom fence rail as the horse nuzzled against her outstretched hand.

"What will happen to Ace and Cal when you're gone," she asked, her voice light in the breeze.

"It'll be John's place. You can help him."

"Will he sit with me in the barn?"

"Maybe, but you'd be okay by yourself."

Jamella ducked between the fence rails, pulling Skip by the sleeve. They stood by the horse, the sun now hidden behind a bank of gray-black clouds. She took his trembling fingers and placed them under Cal's jaw. The old man's hand was cold to the touch. Together, they felt the horse's slow, pulsing heart.

"Let the doctor help you," she said softly.

Skip pressed his lips together.

"Might be too late for that," he said, half-smiling, but knowing he was not going to fight—no machines, no infusions, no special care or treatments. He'd had his time, and what was there to his days anyway? His only companion was a freckled faced, frizzy-haired girl whose tongue was a springboard for *any* idea standing upon it. Skip had been encouraged after Eloise to try again, build a life, but the will was weak, lost. He had taken calls from women, which might have led to more if they had not happened either too soon, too late, or somewhere in between and were never just right.

Eloise, and the easy laugh that had drawn his attention when he had walked across campus long ago, was the only woman who remained in his thoughts after graduation and while in Vietnam. He had formally met her at the college bookstore where she worked stocking shelves and managing inventory. He needed a drafting manual and hoped she might find a used one for him.

"Trying to save a few bucks," he said sheepishly, after she had knocked around in the back of a dusty supply closet to find the edition Skip needed.

"Happens a lot," she said, matter-of-factly while wiping the back of her hand across her forehead, fingertips spotted with gray dust.

"Eloise," he said, reading her nametag. "Different, I like it."

"Me, too. It's old fashioned, but I don't like Elly."

He looked into her light green eyes.

"It fits."

She tipped her head to one side.

"You can tell that by just looking?"

Unlike other women on campus, she didn't wear hippie-chic bellbottom, hip hugger denim jeans, and a cropped top. Instead, she wore a three-quarter sleeved beige blouse and trim fitting pants, with her brown hair curled into waves by the side of her face. They dated for a year, usually capping the night with tea and a pastry at a bakery off campus, until graduation. The understanding was that if he returned, and she was available, they would reconnect.

Eloise liked his calm, his needling sense of humor and the polite, mannered way in which he acted. While she identified with the wave of feminism coursing through campus in the early sixties, she still accepted Skip's gentlemanly deference. She picked the row of seats at a movie, or chose the pastry, while he held the door or helped her with a coat. They would sit by the street window, sharing a cannoli and talking about all that swirled around them, the anti-war movement, Betty Friedan, the assassination of JFK, and civil rights. Skip liked Eloise's practical, even evaluation of facts and events. She was not against his service commitment. Instead, she held that we are the masters of our fates, and our choices were no one's business.

Eloise did worry about Skip's impending deployment, but supported him. Her practicality, her unwillingness to be judgmental made Skip realize she was the one, someone whose fair mindedness and even temper matched his, if only she would be available when he returned. They wrote while he was overseas and, with each note, his anxiety rose. So many "Dear John" letters had fluttered across the ocean that he expected one, too. He would chastise himself in the time between messages, thinking maybe she could wait for one year, but two? An independent, attractive woman was sure to meet someone. So he worried as the end of each month came, hoping not to read, "I hope this letter finds you well."

Skip's replies were not of the war, but of the positives he experienced, either in the beauty of the tropics, or of oddball characters and their antics. He reminded her, too, that he was looking forward to seeing her, but his letters were harder to write as his time wound down. The order, discipline and reasons for fighting and dying wore on him, as did his failure to lead *all* of his men, and his replies were shorter. The positives were gone, so much so that he waited two months after returning stateside before meeting her at the bakery.

He arrived a half hour early, standing by the front door, nervously chewing sticks of mint gum and wondering if he was not a bit out of his mind. He was determined to ask her if she had any real interest in him, but his resolve softened when he saw her approach, smiling, and dressed professionally. Eloise worked in the personnel department of a retail chain and wore a deep green dress belted at the waist with a matching short jacket top.

"Thought you'd never call," she said, teasingly.

Her casual greeting reignited an old familiarity. Skip relaxed and dropped his preplanned words.

"You don't wear name tags at Waldenbooks?"

"Not at the corporate office," she said, hand moving to his forearm. "Only the clerks digging through dusty old books for fussy customers do."

They sat by the window, sharing three chocolate amaretti cookies.

"Are you letting your hair grow out?" she asked, pointing with a piece of cookie at his head.

"I do need a haircut. Shouldn't be a long wait at the barber's by the looks of things."

Eloise smiled.

"Is being home what you expected?"

He looked about the chatty café, noting the tie-dyed shirts, bell sleeved blouses, aviator glasses, and frayed jeans.

Skip said, "In some ways it is, and others it's not. I'm not surprised by the long hair and the anti-war stuff. It was like that overseas, but I am surprised at how nice it is to be here with you, like I'd never left," he said, a smile crossing his lips.

She reached for his hand. Her eyes were soft, and he could feel her warm, thin fingertips against his.

Skip would tell her later of the struggle to adjust so she would understand his moments of quiet, of sadness for a planned career in the military—the rules, the routine, the sense of what to expect and what to do—obliterated into fragments beyond recognition. It would be a while before Skip recognized who he was, what he liked, and how to live in a fashion that suited him. He was grateful Eloise was available when he returned. She accelerated the process.

Being in the café with her now, as if he had never gone to war, gave him hope. He saw a first step.

Squeezing her hand, he said, "I'm happy to be here with you again."

"That's nice," she said, raising the cup to her lips, a smile in her eyes.

After her passing he would, of course, miss Eloise, miss her closeness when in bed, or her warm breath upon his neck. It was obvious to his co-workers, too, who would occasionally bring coffee and a muffin for him, or have a supper to go. Later, they even suggested a friend whom he might like, which he politely declined.

On the Friday afternoon of a Labor Day weekend, he took ten of his colleagues for drinks and sandwiches. After paying the bill, Skip raised his arms to quiet them.

"You've all been great, and I appreciate it. I'm at peace, so thanks," he said, his way of telling them a return to normal around the office was in order.

He preferred to keep his memories of Eloise, to remember how rabbits in the garden drove her crazy or to think of the music they enjoyed instead of finding another partner. Many unexpected moments or thoughts of her would come to him, bringing Skip something to smile at and think about, even though the memory of Eloise would leave him saddened. Something as simple as the smell of coffee reminded Skip of the times they shared desserts when dating long ago.

Skip's reverie was interrupted when he heard Jamella say, "It's strong, huh, the heart? That's good, right?" and so he left for now the happy thoughts of Eloise sitting in the café.

Their palms pulsed against Cal's neck—the elemental threads of life: warmth, touch, light, air, and tenderness—

woven within their fingertips. Cal pressed his face against Jamella's chest, and she hugged the horse, her smile wide, eyes excited, alive.

"Got yourself a friend for life," Skip said, glad for the comfort of her happiness.

"We're a team," she said, rubbing the horse's cheeks. "All of us. We're like family, too."

Skip nodded, thinking of the annoying girl he'd first met. *Never would've guessed that*, but he was grateful. Like spring air flooding into a musty cellar, she had unlocked what had been sealed within him through intent and habit.

Jamella allowed Skip to retrace the steps he had walked with Libby, and he often dreamed of his granddaughter, Eloise, and John, and their lives together. He sometimes lay in bed, face to the morning sun, relaxed, no longer feeling the dawn of a day to be another grind. Forgetting how to make drip coffee, use the washer, or checking the tank for heating oil, were Skip's new concerns. Often he'd sit with Ace in the living room, dreaming with his eyes open, until Jamella called after dinner. Only then would he realize he was hungry or that Ace's water and food bowls were empty. Routine and time, he thought, were what he needed, so he kept pens and pads handy for notes, rather than rely on memory.

"She's really softened him," John said, while he and Laura sat at a faded wicker table on the back porch.

"She is a bit abrasive at times," Laura said, with a laugh. "Like a grinding wheel."

"I'm happy she comes by to help. Let me know if he doesn't seem right. I'll know more after the doctor's visit."

"Are you worried?"

John nodded.

"He was smart to put the property into a trust, but when it comes to his health, he's stubborn. How are your parents?"

"Healthy, as far as I know, but I don't see them often. It's a seven hour drive to Missouri."

John leaned closer to Laura.

"So, how'd you end up here?"

Laura sighed.

"Followed my fiancé, but it fell apart after a year. My fault really. I wanted more than he was willing to offer. I knew that, but hoped it would eventually work out. I decided that since I'd established a business, I stuck around. Hard enough to get one business off the ground never mind another. The truth though was I didn't want to face my parents or my sisters, so I stayed. My parents came for an extended visit, but I was happy when they left. Sometimes distance is better when things don't work out."

"I felt that way. I was a mess for a long time. Worked on the road—became a traveling salesman—so I could hide, really. Then too much alcohol," he said, raising a mug of tea. "Had to clean up. I was okay at work, but alone, not so much. My dad's advice was to keep going, one foot in front of the other," John paused, defeat shining in his eyes.

"It's hard work carrying a heavy heart."

John nodded.

Even though Skip kept on, it had not been easy for the old man, either. As time stretched between father and son, Skip wondered what he had done, and grew tired of John's one word answers. Overtime, it seemed there was no commonness at all. Why push what can't be moved?

"So," Laura said softly, hands flat on the table. "Here we all are."

14

Lucia waited on the sidewalk before nine a.m. Sunday morning, feeling free, finally. While her brother was a godsend, she needed to be on her own, alone, watching cars and saying "Hello," to those who walked past. She wiggled her arms and took deep breaths like a swimmer on a race platform, as she waited at the bus stop. Lucia sipped convenience store coffee, her eyes squinting against the bright, spring morning light. In her pocket, she had placed a neatly folded list of items to buy at discount box stores: underwear, socks, a zip up hoodie, lightweight work tees and pants, and a good pair of sneakers.

Familiar faces joined her on the bus, but she dismissed the notion as impossible. She had been away too long and much had changed with the neighborhood, but still she wondered about the older riders who caught her eye. While she rode, though, the idea of being the one who *went to jail* tempered her optimism. How would she react if asked? It had never been an issue for her to admit a mistake, her guilt, but the grief she had caused shamed and saddened her. Lucia turned to the window and ignored riders. Stepping from the bus, she sighed and focused on the slip of paper in her pocket.

Head down, she walked the plaza from one discount store to the next, finding the best she could afford. Like other shoppers, she was more interested in what she could buy rather than who bought what and the apprehension of being recognized faded.

By noon, she had finished. Hungry, she sat at the bus stop, wishing she could visit one of the fast food restaurants lining the parking lot, but she did not want to carry shopping bags, so she opted to wait. It had been good to be alone and to see how much more there was of everything—stores, restaurants, coffee shops, cars, and trucks—but people hadn't changed. Those with little money hunted for bargains and drove cars that rattled and burned oil, while others drove sports utility vehicles and shopped at upscale stores. In that sense, it was the world she remembered, and she was hopeful.

Her past would always be a part of the present but as Mrs. Gomez had often said, "Use your past to make new dreams," which brought a smile to Lucia.

When she had asked how Tina remained positive, she replied, "The world is full of people who know what's wrong with *everything*. I'd rather ignore them and be happy."

Lucia would hold that thought through the day, while washing new clothes, making sandwiches for herself and Jesus for Monday, and listening to a newly purchased transistor radio.

At dusk, she stood on the back porch looking out over the neighborhood, watching as others came and went, talked and laughed. She would put no beer in the refrigerator or buy cigarettes—bad habits to avoid—and not get a car unless she found full-time certified nurse's assistant work. In the darkness, neighboring apartment lights flashed on and off like fireflies. Lucia was content.

While she would later wake some nights with anxious, chaotic dreams of prison, she could wipe those away with the belief that each day was a step to a better future, and the dreams would eventually disappear. She also needed to hold back the guilt and disappointment of her past; a flash flood of emotion that stole Lucia's breath.

Above on the flat tar roof, doves cooed softly, almost in whispers.

"What is it? What don't you want me to know?" She smiled.

Not bad, she thought, as the evening air chilled her hands and toes, for a true first day.

Jamella's Sunday was disappointing. Her "Please Don't Litter" sign was flattened, torn, and covered with wide tire tracks.

"That's not good," Skip said to Jamella, her face flushed with hurt. "But I got an idea. Interested?"

When she nodded, he added, "Go tell your mom you'll be here all day painting. Meet me in the barn."

Jamella later returned dressed in a worn, multi-colored clown outfit and holding cloth work gloves.

"Now that's interesting," Skip said, resting on one knee and stirring a can of white paint.

"My old Halloween suit. It's plasticky," Jamella said, "so the paint won't stick."

"Makes sense. So, you're an artist right? Think you can use this to make a sign?"

Jamella looked at the four-foot by four foot piece of smooth plywood leaning against the barn door.

"Yes," she said, smiling. "That will make a huge sign!"

"Good," the old man said, rising from one knee. "Ever use a paint roller? We'll cover it with white paint and then letter it."

He guided her on pouring fast drying latex paint into a roller tray, cleaning the drip from the side of the can with a brush, and then wetting the fuzzy roller.

"Nice and even," he said, his shaky cold hand upon hers. "Don't spread it too thin."

Jamella refilled the paint tray three times before finishing.

"Where do you find these clowns?" John said, standing with a bag of groceries near the barn entrance.

"Ha, ha," Jamella said. "Forgot to laugh."

"Wonder where she picked up that wisecrack," John said to Skip. "So, what's all this?"

"Somebody crushed my sign. This one's going to be huge!"

After lunch, while Laura and Jamella finished the lettering, Skip and John dug two post holes and sunk two stakes along the road to support the sign.

John finished digging the three-feet needed to support one pole before Skip had dug down a foot. The old man struggled to drive the shovel into the ground and, when he tried to stand on the spade to force it deeper, he would stumble to one side.

At one point, he fell to his knees. John pretended not to notice.

Skip rose, cursed under his breath, then took another stab at the hole.

"Looks like you hit some rocks," John said, trying to spare his dad from embarrassment. "I don't know where you want the stakes. Why don't you handle that while I finish the hole?"

John easily finished the digging, but Skip struggled with the small sledgehammer. He was too weak to hold the wood stake in one hand and swing the top-heavy tool with the other, often missing it entirely and slamming the mallet into the dirt.

Finally, Skip went down to his knees, head down, hands on thighs, too tired to continue.

Again, John ignored his father's troubles but did ask Skip to hold the round wooden post upright so John could set it into place.

As they worked, the old man's jaw hung open and his breathing was heavy, uneven.

The white and blue lettered sign was in place by five in the afternoon with Jamella banging the last nail into the two-by-four bracing.

It read, "Please Don't Litter! Thank You! (2)"

"The two means it's the second one," Jamella said, proudly.

"And hopefully, the last," Laura said, hands and forehead blotched with blue paint.

John used his cell phone to take a picture of the four of them standing by the sign.

"What do you think?" he asked Jamella of the snap shot on his phone. "Looks good to me."

The girl nodded.

"It's like we're a family."

Skip placed his shaky hand upon the girl's head.

"And don't forget Cal and Ace," he said.

"Yup, we need a picture with them, too," she said, taking Skip's hand and leading him back to the barn.

John turned to Laura, her face smudged, hair streaked and curled with sweat against her neck and said, "Who is that kid and what has she done with my dad?"

"She's full of surprises," Laura said, her eyes shining proudly.

They stood for a moment, neither speaking.

"It's really nice," John said softly, as if meant only for him.

"Are we talking about the sign or the two of them?" Laura said.

"Both. I do tend to infer two things at once, huh?"

They laughed, eyes lingering on each other. "You keep me on my toes at least," Laura said.

They each grabbed a shovel, while John grabbed the hammer.

Extending his arm to Laura he said, "Come on. Even non-union workers get a dinner break."

Laura laughed, as she slipped her free arm through his. The day's work and fatigue had made them silly.

"I like where this is going," she said.

"Me, too. Wait. Do you mean walking up the driveway or—"

"Oh, please. Knock it off, okay?" She squeezed his arm tightly. "I'm too pooped to keep this going."

On Monday morning, Lucia met the four Hispanic men Jesus had contracted to paint the apartment complex.

"We'll finish this in two weeks," he said.

"Are they your employees?"

"No. They're self-employed subcontractors. They follow the work, not the boss. I schedule them in advance."

He introduced her, saying "My little sister, Gloria." Then the men fell into a familiar routine. Lucia's job was to keep the paint buckets full of white primer, which was sprayed evenly and quickly upon the ceiling and walls. She spoke little to the men who wore white zip-up disposable coveralls and respirators. A radio with a bent antenna and crusty paint blotches blasted music as the men sprayed wands of paint over the sheetrock. Lucia hustled to keep their buckets filled with paint.

At lunch, she said to her brother, "This is going so fast!" Jesus smiled.

"And that's how we make money."

Lucia was tired after the first two days but settled into the work as the week wore on.

The men were diligent, focused and not inclined to chitchat, which was fine with Lucia, who was happy to work, to be busy, to have nothing to think about but pouring gallons of paint into buckets.

On Thursday after work, she introduced herself to the first and second floor tenants in her building which consisted of Latino, Asian, and African-American college students. Each apartment was a four-bedroom, two-bath open floor plan suite with common dining and living room areas. The students were polite, friendly and surprisingly neat.

"For sure," Jesus said later. "I only rent to the serious ones. They like it that way, and when one goes, they find another."

For Lucia, it had been a good first week. As each day passed, she was immersed in work and with the rituals of everyday life—cleaning, laundry, cooking, or putting one's feet up. Lucia's new life emerged. Like opening a tight fist, her anxiety about the future eased. If painting with Jesus was her future, she was content.

Jamella was ready Saturday night with binoculars and a Tracfone. As soon as Laura went to sleep, Jamella tiptoed to the second floor hall window to watch the sign, which was slightly visible from the nearest street lamp two houses away. She was determined to learn who was leaving trash and planned to rest her eyes for two minutes and use the binoculars for eight. Jamella was satisfied with the plan but sometime after midnight, she lost the battle with her heavy eyelids and fell asleep, head resting against the wall under the windowsill.

Two hours later, she woke with a start, rubbed her eyes and looked. No trash, so she resumed her watch then rest routine.

Just as her eyelids grew heavy again, a dual-wheeled truck with two dirt bikes secured to its bed stopped, lights off, by the sign. A small bodied, shorthaired figure stepped out from the passenger side, took a large-handled plastic barrel from the back and quietly dumped its contents. Jamella pressed the preprogrammed police department phone number and described the truck to the dispatcher.

"What's the plate number?"

With one eye peering through the lens she said, "Looks like, 7-7-1-7-8."

"All right. We'll send a car now."

With her elbows on the windowsill, she watched through the binoculars as the passenger hopped into the front cabin and closed the truck door. The vehicle moved forward, frustrating Jamella, as she thought the police would be too late, but it stopped.

Instead of leaving, the driver turned and backed into the sign, digging its wheels into the roadside sand. The wooden posts and sign bent under the weight of the rear fender, cracking and snapping.

"No!" Jamella said.

She ran down the stairs and grabbed a jacket. She flew out, leaving the front door open. Jamella heard the plywood sign break in two, as the posts and supports cracked and tangled under the truck body. Its rear wheels spun, pitching dirt and rock into Skip's yard, but it couldn't move forward to leave. Once more the tires whirled, firing chunks of wood and rock far into the darkness, but it was stuck.

The whoop of a siren accompanied by blue and white flashing lights stopped the truck's engine. The patrol car's spotlight shone on two faces in the front cab, each with a hand up by their eyes.

Laura spotted Jamella, her form black against the bright light.

"I called it in," she said in a formal, procedural voice.

Laura chuckled despite the seriousness of the moment.

A second police car stopped behind the first. Soon the officers had the riders alongside the first cruiser, hands upon the truck's hood.

Skip and Ace came to the edge of the driveway and stood with Laura and Jamella.

"Isn't this something," Skip commented, as two state police cruisers arrived.

He wore a gray wool coat over a pair of blue and red checked flannel pajama pants.

"Thought there was an accident—"

"They smashed the sign on purpose!" the girl said, hands on hips.

Sergeant Wilson conferred with the other officers, then spoke to Skip.

"Your sign, right?" he asked Skip.

"It's my sign," Jamella said.

"On my property."

"So, we've got a juvenile and the driver, who's under the influence. Tow truck's coming to impound the vehicle. We'll jam him up for vandalism, too."

"Good!" Skip said. "They've been making a mess for months."

"You'll probably get a couple of hundred in restitution," Wilson said, before walking away.

"Ah," Skip said, "maybe we'll plant a tree there."

Turning to leave, Jamella said with surprise, "I think one of them is a girl!"

"Girls do stupid things, too," Laura said, shaking her head.

They walked away unaware of the driver's angry scowl from the backseat of the cruiser.

15

"I've been getting lots of texts about you, Little Sister," Jesus said, Monday morning as they were pulling on their paint coveralls. "Lots of interested men."

"They learned about my painting skills?"

"Or maybe how sexy you look in coveralls."

Lucia smiled.

"Sure. That's it."

"I can recommend someone if you want."

"I know the clock is ticking," she said, zipping up the front, "but I'm not ready."

Jesus moved closer so the others on the site would not hear.

"These men won't be interested forever."

Lucia squinted, her brain working.

Finally, she said, "Did you make a bet on which one of these guys would be my first date?"

Jesus laughed.

"Oh, no. No."

"Liar!" Lucia punched his arm. "Hope you lose."

Later in the morning, though, she did notice a new laborer with no wedding band. He worked hard and kept to himself. She knew not wearing a ring meant nothing since he might be living with someone or, like Jesus, preferred to have lady friends. The long ago hope of a home and family tugged at Lucia. If only she had been more focused then, she might have both now.

She had chided herself many times for wanting only to have friends and money in her pocket, but the reality of what might have been grew as she settled into this life. She thought of the white woman, Laura, and the adopted child. Would her future come to that? Most of the men Lucia knew were married or had some type of clingy past to worry her. What awaited her? What might she uncover?

Instead of waiting to find out, she tapped on a man's forearm and introduced herself. She liked how he politely took the five gallon paint bucket from her hands, and the softness of his brown eyes.

"Andres," he said, with almost no Spanish accent. "But your brother calls me Andy."

Jesus later explained that Andres had worked in an American hotel in Guatemala City, and he wired money back home to his wife and son.

"He's been in the U.S. for five months and hopes to be a citizen when his green card expires. Why? You like him?"

Lucia's cheeks reddened.

"He has a family."

Jesus lit a cigarette. They were outside during a break for lunch, sitting on pails in the shade of a concrete wall.

"So?" he said, without smiling. "I'm sure he'd like some company."

"No. That's not for me."

"Why not?" Jesus said. "You should have a little happiness, a little fun."

Jesus exhaled, the white smoke trailing off in the breeze.

"Time to make your own rules."

When Lucia didn't reply he added, "Won't hurt to ask."

"Don't you dare," she said, grabbing his arm. "I mean it."

Lucia spent the afternoon adjusting to the idea of getting what she wanted. Prison had locked her into the past along with memories of the flirting and silliness she had dallying with boys, as she now saw them, not men. Now, at thirty-eight years old, the game was simpler, no silly chitchat, and the prize easier to win.

Later Andres would tell her, "There's little future back home. I did have a good job, but I make more in two days here," an unintentional reminder to Lucia of the chances she had squandered.

He spoke of how American hotel guests had so much, not just in money or clothes, but in the expectation of a good life. He overheard talk of interesting jobs, college educations, music lessons, and select soccer leagues for children.

"You can live a life of hope here," he said, as he walked to his used, white Dodge van. "Back home it is very difficult with no *educación*."

"But you speak well for no school."

He laughed.

"Watched American television programs."

Lucia, nodding at the variety of tools sitting on racks and electrical cords dangling from hooks inside the cargo box, asked, "Is that what you do after work?"

"Yes, little jobs, handyman things. Why? You need some work done?"

This was her opening to flirt, to say with a wink, "Yeah, I *do* need some work done," but she paused, letting the idea roll around in her mind.

She smiled.

"No," she said, "but it would be nice to talk again."

"Sure," he said, taking the ignition key from his pocket. "See you tomorrow."

Lucia stood as the van's engine sprung to life. The idea of intimacy was exciting, but she needed to know there would be trust, too.

Sunday afternoon, Skip and John wanted to remove the broken sign, but Jamella begged them not to.

"I want people to see how it was broken."

"Looks like hell," Skip said.

"That's why we should leave it," the girl said. "Bad stuff happens but people forget."

"So true," John said, shovel in hand. "Guess this can wait."

"Let's go find Cal," Skip said.

Jamella and Hannah ran up the driveway, with a tail wagging Ace, ears flopping, in pursuit.

"That was an interesting thought," John said.

"Yup," Skip said, walking with shoulders stooped and head down. "No rush to repair it."

"No. She's right. Bad things happen and then they are forgotten."

"She's smart for a kid. Sees everything."

John chuckled.

"Like Santa, huh?"

"Nah. Like God."

John placed his hand on Skip's shoulder.

"Wow, that's high praise from a guy who didn't want her around."

Skip wiped at the spit at the side of his mouth.

"It's easy to be wrong."

"Sure is," John said. "Why are you hunched over? You're like a walking question mark. Up straight, Lieutenant."

Skip tilted his head back and with chin out, swung his arms like a soldier on parade.

"That's it," John said. "Now you can work for the circus scooping elephant poop."

Skip saluted.

"Thanks for the tip."

John looked forward to meeting with Skip's primary care doctor on Monday, but a medical complication occurred later that afternoon when Skip fell to one knee clutching his chest. He went down as he reached for the back door.

John initially thought the old man had bent to tie his shoe but saw the strained muscles of his face and neck. He could hear Jamella talking on her Tracfone to an emergency operator.

Thank God for that kid!

"He needs to chew aspirin," Jamella shouted, as she ran with Hannah from the barn. "The rescue's coming."

"Hold on, Dad," John said, leaving Skip curled and gasping against the porch railing.

Above the kitchen sink, John found a bottle of coated aspirin. The orange pills were small and hard. Placing them on the counter, he crushed two tablets under the weight of a heavy ceramic mug, then whisked them into his hand. He ran through the open kitchen door to find Jamella, her face furrowed in determination, pressing both hands against Skip's chest, at the direction of the emergency operator. John dropped the powdery aspirin into the old man's mouth and watched it dissolve on his tongue.

"Let's switch," he said to Jamella, taking over the compressions.

Jamella sat against the back of her legs.

"His lips are turning blue," she said into the phone, "Where are they?"

Hannah's eyes were wide, and her jaw hung. It was only her second playdate with Jamella, and she was shaken by Skip's struggle with pain.

Laura was pulling clothes from the dryer when she heard sirens. When the sound didn't fade, she went to the window to see the flashing lights of a police cruiser, ambulance, and fire truck climb Skip's driveway. Concerned for her daughter, she ran out the back door, slipping and sliding in flip-flops as she negotiated the hill behind the barn.

Winded, she paused at the top, her cheek stinging from the swipe of a tree branch. She spotted Jamella standing next to John, and two female EMT's kneeling by Skip, who was sitting on the porch. Her relief was tempered by the site of Skip placed onto a gurney and rolled to the open back door of the ambulance.

They tightened the straps holding the old man before lifting him into the ambulance.

"Can you lock up for me?" John asked.

The women nodded.

"Call me," Laura said.

Laura went inside to lock the house while Jamella brought Ace's water and food bowls into the barn. Laura wiped the kitchen counter. She turned a light on by the sink before leaving. Locking the door, she hurried to the barn. It was time to take Hannah home.

The girls sat with Ace, watching as Cal chewed strands of hay.

Jamella said confidently, "He'll be alright. Don't worry."

Hannah nodded, as they sat tucked into the dark shadows of soft, fading light.

Laura turned away, remembering how Hannah had stood to the side while Jamella stayed with Skip.

Leaning against the outside of the dry, faded barn door, Laura waited, pleased as Jamella gave Hannah comfort. Laura knew that Hannah's grandfather had died peacefully one June morning while seated on the back porch rocker. Unfortunately, Hannah was the first to discover the old man, coffee spilled and wet on his lap. Thinking he had fallen asleep, she tried to rouse him. The sudden arrival of emergency personnel was a sharp reminder of her grandfather's death.

"His passing changed her," Hannah's mom told Laura. "I mean she was always a quiet kid, but since then she's drifted into reading constantly—which isn't bad, I guess. I'm glad she wants to spend time with your daughter."

Jamella and Hannah stood with Cal, hands on his warm side flank.

Life goes on, Laura thought, but it does leave a rutted trail behind.

Laura, too, hoped Skip would recover. Looking at the house, yard, and field, she wasn't ready to let it go. The property, its grumpy owner—and son—had changed her. She liked having John to talk to, to share observations about Jamella, Skip, and work but was unsure if they would ever be more than friends. John was, though, a possibility...an intriguing one.

She called to the girls, "Ready?"

Laura secured the door, while Ace barked and whimpered behind it.

The next morning, Jamella would find Ace sleepy-eyed and laying on hay bales near Cal's stall.

Skip had suffered a mild heart attack, which would have been good news if it were not for the complications discovered after his hospital admission.

"He'll be transferred to a rehabilitation facility for further observation," the admitting doctor said. "Aside from a failing heart, he may have a combination of Parkinson's and heart failure, and they can put a care plan together. No matter what, though, he's at the point where some everyday help, long-term, is needed."

"You mean like in a nursing home?" John said to the Asian physician with short cropped, black hair.

"In-home should be fine for now," she added. "He will have plenty of meds to take, which have to be monitored daily, and his overall health needs watching, too. Is he eating? Breathing well, things like that?"

John sighed.

"Breathing well?"

"Heart failure and Parkinson's can cause fluid to build in the lungs."

"Doesn't sound good. So, he's dying. Geez, how long?"

"I usually wait for the full medical to decide, but it is time to plan. His heart could give out any day. In fact, it already has, but he'll be under observation for a few days, so you have time to decide on what's best."

After the doctor left, John said, "Did you hear that?" to Skip who was asleep in the hospital bed, lying flat on his back, a slight, gurgling snore coming with each lifting of his chest.

John stood by the fourth-floor window, the streets quiet near midnight, and felt the heavy tug for a gin and tonic. Instead, he called Laura.

Realizing it was past midnight, he was about to drop the call when she answered.

"Sorry, Laura. I just realized how late—"

"How's your dad?"

"Stable, but he'll need lots of help. In-home care for a while, at least."

"And how are you?"

John paused.

The dishonesty of saying he was "fine" stuck in his throat.

"If you hadn't picked up, I might've stopped for a drink."

"It *was* a long day."

So many thoughts of his father, his care and the guilt he felt for drifting apart from Skip tangled John's tongue. He heard Laura breathing softly through the phone. Her patience calmed him.

Finally, he said, "Thanks for listening."

"Let's talk tomorrow. Jamella and I want to help."

After ending the call, he looked beyond the glare of the city lights, following the highway to the suburbs and to Laura's home. He patted his father's feet as a goodbye. Walking to the parking garage, he pushed the thoughts of the day from his mind to think of Laura. His call to her had been instinctive, his first thought.

16

In time, Lucia thought of prison as reawakening from a long coma. She enjoyed the privacy of the apartment, where, without a cellmate, she could be alone with her thoughts and not have to consider the dynamics of life behind bars. She could have a male friend, Andres, to talk with on lunch breaks. Thankfully, Jesus found "errands" to run, so Lucia could sit with Andres and notice how he smiled, what he ate, or how clean he kept his hands.

Andres was unwrapping a peanut butter and jelly sandwich when Lucia had the sense of awakening from a long sleep.

Her skin tingled, and she smiled.

"What?" he asked.

"Is that your favorite?"

"Ha, yes. Easy and cheap. Want half?"

She shook her head.

A man, she thought, not a silly boy, and a door opened. Conversations about their childhoods, the silliness of their younger selves, their mistakes and hopes cheered Lucia.

She would find someone. She told him of the car accident and of her time in prison, while he explained the scar on his right chin and of the missing tooth.

"Fighting to stay out of the gangs," he said. "That life—guns, money, *chicas locas*—was not for me. My father was proud. I learned. This life here, in America, is *muy mejorar*, you know? Way better."

They sat on overturned paint pails, work boots splotched with paint, and hair matted with sweat. Lucia opened a plastic container with sliced strawberries and offered them.

He looked into her eyes, and they held each other's attention.

"I know you have a wife," she said. "but could we be friends? Maybe have dinner?"

Andres pressed his lips together, his groomed black beard bunching at his mouth.

"Would your brother approve?"

Lucia blinked rapidly.

"He wants me to have, uh, fun."

Andres nodded, but didn't respond.

"I need someone I can trust," Lucia said. *To help me feel like a woman.* "Do you know a nice place?"

"Like shirt and tie nice?"

She smiled.

"Yes."

"I'll make reservations for Friday night. Do you mind going in the van? Not a very special ride."

Lucia thought of the dark, tight dress she had tried on at a discount clothing store. Too sexy, but the small flower print one would do.

"So, yes?"

Lucia's eyes widened.

"I'd like that," and the remaining two workdays were long for her in anticipation of their dinner date.

Neither of them spoke much of it except for the logistics of time, and what was on the menu, but she was excited.

Lucia kept her emotions to herself, not wanting to appear eager, or worse, desperate. She, too, fought the urge to make sandwiches of chicken and beans for him, or to sew on new buttons to replace those missing from his work shirts. He is not my boyfriend, she reminded herself, but the tingling sense of having one someday soon filled her lungs with a freshness that quickly put open space between her past and present.

"So big date tonight, huh?" Jesus teased as they drove home.

"Did you win the bet?"

"No. Andy was the favorite so no one would bet against him."

"Pretty obvious," she said, stepping from the van. "He was the only gentleman. Thanks for the ride."

"Next week we start a new job—no Andres," Jesus said. "Try not to be too sad. It's the house with the little girl."

When Andres arrived, Lucia was waiting on the porch, deliberately looking in the opposite direction. From the corner of her eye, she saw the van at the curb and heard the groan of the driver's door when it opened.

"Oh!" she said, feigning surprise.

"You look nice," Andres said, of her knee length flowered dress.

She wore a bit of eyeliner, lip-gloss and Lucia's dark hair rested upon her shoulders.

"Thank you," she said, to Andres who wore a plain white shirt with no loose buttons, blue tie, and new blue jeans. "We're presentable, at least."

As they approached the steak house restaurant, Andres asked, "Should I let a valet park the van?"

Lucia laughed.

"Only if you trust them with it."

"Better not take the chance," he said, turning into another, free parking lot.

They sat at a quiet corner table.

Lucia was floored by the al la carte menu prices.

"Twelve dollars for a baked potato?"

Andres' eyes twinkled in the low light.

"It comes with a surprise, like Cracker Jacks."

Lucia drank a strawberry margarita while Andres had, "What I came here for, a Gallo. Few places serve the favorite beer of Guatemala. I usually sit at the bar and have one. It's a bit much to come here often. And you like margaritas?"

Lucia shrugged.

"Wanted to order something fancy. It's good, though."

She watched as waiters wearing white shirts, black pants, and bolo ties went from table to table opening wine bottles, bringing plates of food, or cleaning crumbs from linen tablecloths.

"Very impressive," she said, of the shiny wood veneer bar and half walls. "This is much more than I expected. Thank you."

Over chopped salads and medium-well sirloin steak dinners, Andres spoke of his wife, Carmel, two-year-old son Marcus, and his mother who lives with them. Either the *pisto* I send will get them here, or we'll find a better place to live there. Most likely there. It's very hard to get into the U.S. now, or become a citizen."

It was the first sign of exasperation or bitterness in Andres since they'd met, but he explained the positive side by saying, "The money is much better. Save, save, it's our only chance."

Lucia spoke of prison and her guilt.

"I woke many times thinking it was a bad dream. I had been so careless."

Andres did not interrupt or offer sympathy. When finished, she grew silent, her eyes focused on the nearly empty glass held between her hands. Lucia felt the gentle, dreamy tilt of alcohol upon her tongue.

The waiter offered coffee, but Andres requested the check.

"Mistakes are made," he said when they were alone. "As sure as the sun sets."

Later, they sat across from each other in Lucia's living room.

"I'm twenty-nine," Andres said. "Been married for six years. We tried to save before Marcus came, but it went too slow. We both work and *mi madre* watches our son."

It was late, and Lucia felt the energy of their night out fading.

She said good night to him at her apartment door, and asked, "Were you hoping for more?"

He shrugged.

With a smile he said, "I'm glad you didn't make me decide."

Lucia liked his square chin and his sense of mischief brought a smile to her lips. He could easily have been the one, she thought, and was the type she hoped to meet.

"But it was a nice night out," he said. "Should we do it again?"

She nodded.

"Just not so fancy."

Lucia leaned onto her toes and kissed his cheek.

"Thank you."

Later, while washing, her eyes flashed in the sink mirror. *My Oreos. Papa.* She shook her head.

"Not tonight, please."

17

Skip was released on Tuesday, but John was unable to secure a home health care aide, so he moved into his old bedroom.

Nothing remained from his childhood, except an old baseball glove left on a closet shelf, the leather stiff and dry. He was not much for sports, preferring instead to spend his time among the horses, cleaning the barn, feeding the chickens, and riding horses with his friends along the property trails. His parent's twelve acres ran parallel to over fifty acres of wild forest owned by the state so he would take a horse out for hours following narrow deer trails.

In high school, he would drink beer with his friends by a pond accessible from a dirt parking lot. John was sure it was still used by teens for late night parties, especially on Fridays. He would give rides to girls, enjoying the feel of their soft breasts pressed against his back. The girls liked his horse more than they liked him, but he was happy to oblige.

He sat on his childhood bed, looking through the window to the barn, thinking of his uncomplicated younger years. Leaning back, head on a dusty pillow, he smiled. This was his do-over, his chance. He thought of Laura, and didn't want to rush, but everything was easy with her. A lunch date with her and Jamella would be a good place to start.

His first priorities were to find someone to stay with Skip, since he only had five days of accrued vacation time, and John would use it to move most of his belongings to Skip's. Although the old man's affairs were in order, John was not ready for his father to go. He did feel a son's love for Skip, but he needed his father, too, because they shared the same grief. When Skip passed, John alone would carry the burden of tragedy, and it would continue to isolate him as it had all along.

Grief, and John's anger, had caused Carol to leave. His moodiness and irritability had drained her. He struggled at work to be patient. When alone, he lost it, mostly banging on the dashboard of his car when a contract or client fell off his list. At home, it was harder. John felt Carol blamed him, even when she said he was ridiculous.

"How could anyone have expected something like that?" she had said.

Logically, she was right, but guilt took its toll. John was sullen, ill humored, and stuck in, "A mess of your own making," Carol had said.

John could only process her comment as an accusation of guilt, a product of the sadness and self-hate he wouldn't let go.

In later years, he would understand Carol was offering him hope, a way to keep them together, but he had been too guilt struck to recognize it, and that, too, eventually piled onto his self-loathing. He had held on to hate as punishment causing a marriage to die. Then, letting the past go would mean Libby and his mom were forever gone.

He looked up at the ceiling fan, and tried to toss a sock onto a blade, a game he had played many times. The first balled one hit the bottom of the fan and clumps of gray dust scattered and fell softly, like loose down. The second attempt left the sock hanging off the end and he smiled. *Only took two tries!*

The simple act of tossing socks allowed John to step back in time. Had he not known better, he was sixteen again, wondering about everything and anything a young man does, without burden or grief. If only life could be so simple.

Carol had excited and aroused him, but it was only after they had married did he learn what she really wanted or who she was, which changed over time.

With Laura, although there was an attraction, it was an enticing sense of calm, of being grounded, settled, that he craved. Would he have felt this way about Laura if not for Libby standing in front of a telephone pole and saving his life? Would he have come to his dad's aid and even cared for Laura and a mixed-race child had it not been for Libby helping him reanimate his day-to-day? Of course not, he would probably be dead, or disabled after the crash. While logic told him seeing Libby was a coincidence, his heart felt otherwise.

The sock fell, finally, onto the bed at the same time he heard Skip's voice from the kitchen, rousing John. He found Skip wiping a dish at the sink, talking alone. He wanted to tease his old man about talking to his invisible friends but hesitated, deciding to listen. Skip was debating with an imaginary person about flag waving.

"No, you should make them stop, Lieutenant Lowell! You're the skipper in charge."

Skip, eyes squinted, said, "I can't Benny, orders from higher up."

He added, after flipping the ceramic bowl onto a shelf into the cupboard, "Well, yes. I know it's wrong."

"Finishing the dishes?" John asked casually. Skip had gained enough strength since his hospital release to be out of bed, but only for as long as his energy allowed.

Skip turned, scuffing his foot on the floor mat and tipping forward, placing a hand against the table for balance.

"What?" he said.

"I'll be staying here for a while longer, until you're better."

With two hands on the table, he nodded, "Sure, suit yourself."

"Are you dizzy?"

"Yeah."

He then sat, scanning the table as if searching for lost car keys or a wallet.

"I have these dreams. I don't know if I'm awake or asleep."

"You're awake now. Don't worry."

"Eloise, Libby. They visit me."

"Oh? How's that?" John said, not sure of how much to indulge Skip.

He shrugged.

"It's like they've never left."

An unnerving sense of time winding down caused John to understand that death had now set Skip's path. This is it, he thought, like Buster, my first beagle. The dog, tail wagging, would wait for John and the afternoon school bus until it didn't. Then, poof, there was no Buster sitting excitedly at the end of the driveway. Those days without the dog were untethered and lonely. Someday, too, the house would be empty. Skip's placing of one foot in front of the other had brought him to within steps of the grave.

"Seeing Mom...is that a good thing?"

"I believe so," he said. "She gives me peace."

"Good," John said, thinking of Libby standing with a bike on the side of the highway. "Maybe there is something to this afterlife business after all."

He helped Skip walk back to the recliner.

Once seated, Skip said, "Sounds like you're changing your tune. I'm right about that—not the religion side, but heaven and hell. You'll see."

John placed a light wool comforter on Skip's legs.

"I'll probably get a good look at hell then. Now rest," John said, turning off the side table lamp.

"That's why that little girl is here," Skip said. "Miss J, I call her. I know it was Libby's doing. She was with us that day when Miss J came for the trash out front."

John nodded and wanted to ask, "Why Libby? Why now?" but Skip was dying and needed help. Could eternity and those who enter it still care about those left behind?

For John, a non-believer, the thought was comforting. He had never been one for church service and the rituals, but it was nice to think there might be an angel, Libby, on their shoulders.

"It's nice to have them," Skip said, head back, eyes closed. "Feel better than ever."

John went to the basement, plastic laundry basket in hand. Libby would be twenty-eight, and John would probably be a grandfather, or not. Libby was happy, focused, and a serious student who enjoyed school. Her adult self, family or career path, though, were forever unknown. John pushed these ideas aside as he pulled warm clothes from the dryer. We can be anything or nothing, he thought, and John had been both. It was time now, to make his future.

18

On a sleepy Monday morning bus ride to school, Jamella sat with Hannah, who was two chapters into a fantasy novel about a black-cowled reaper.

"Someone who comes to gather the souls of the dead. It's scary, but I like it," Hannah explained, when two eighth grade boys shuffled on at the last stop before school.

Hoods over their heads, they paused, white faces hidden in shadow.

"Smells bad today," one said to the other, leaning and sniffing near Jamella's head.

"Or like a snitch," said the other, standing near Hannah, who kept her eyes to the paperback open in her lap. "Yeah, it's the shit stain that smells. You know who that is, right?" he continued, forcefully pushing the back of Jamella's head.

"What's going on, Mike," said Judy, the bus driver, watching the two through a rectangular rear-view mirror.

"Nothing," Mike said, "just stinks like crap right here."

As Judy watched, Hannah lifted a wintergreen Lifesaver and stuck it in Mike's face.

"Here. Use this, butt breath."

The boy wanted to slap it away but knew better.

"Keep moving, Mister Clean," Judy said with the raspy hoarseness of a lifelong cigarette smoker.

"Want to make a big deal about a sign, huh?" Mike said under his breath, as he walked to his seat in the rear. "My cousin's going to get you."

At that, Jamella's pencil stopped scratching against the thick art pad. She had not thought about those who had ruined it. Why would someone bother her for doing what was right? Wasn't that what she was taught to do?

Mike and his dopey friend, Kevin, two acne-addled jerks, would push and shove in line, slap kids behind the head, swear, steal, and tease anyone who wasn't perfect. Homely and long-limbed, they enjoyed hurting those who would not push back.

Hannah, though, was unafraid.

As they walked off the bus, she handed a note to the driver. At afternoon dismissal, Mike was not on the bus.

"He's off for a week," Judy said to Hannah. "Suspension from riding won't change him, but we'll get a break."

"Why aren't you drawing?" Hannah asked Jamella, who sat with her hands folded.

Jamella sighed.

"Don't feel like it. I'm going to ask Mister Skip about the sign stuff. I didn't do anything wrong. And I'm going to ask if you can come visit Cal again on Saturday. Is that okay?"

Hannah smiled.

Jamella arrived to find Laura, Jesus and Gloria standing in the living room.

"We'll be here tomorrow, mid-morning," Jesus said, holding a partial payment check with Laura's signature. "Maybe three days, four at most, to finish. Oh, and you should let the local police know. They're not used to seeing me in a neighborhood like this."

Gloria stood with a notepad and small chart of color swatches.

"Nice to see you again," Gloria said to Jamella. "Would you like to pick the color of your room? Here, this is what mom likes. It's sort of a dark blue."

"Starting trouble, huh?" Jesus said with a smirk.

Jamella picked a lighter shade, and Laura nodded.

"Good choice."

Jamella handed the color swatches to Gloria. Holding the woman's hand, Jamella ran her fingers gently in a circle upon Gloria's skin, slowly moving over the knuckles then to the fingertips.

"Your hands are dry," she said softly, eyes trained upon Gloria's skin.

"I have lotion in the van."

"Must be a cheap kind," Jamella said, still holding Gloria's fingers.

Gloria agreed.

"I should buy something better."

"I can't draw if I can't understand something," Jamella said with conviction. "Or if I feel unsure."

"Unsure?" Gloria asked, her fingertips touching the girls.

"Yeah, with what's really going on inside," she said, looking into Gloria's eyes. "Your heart is full of stuff, huh?"

"It is," she said, forcing a smile. "You're perceptive."

"I *am* an artist," Jamella said smartly, releasing Gloria's hand.

"Mister Skip," Jamella asked, during Cal's evening feeding, "what are the police doing about the sign?"

Skip, seated on a bale of hay, blew on his hands.

"Raw today. Can't keep my hands warm."

"Mister Skip, did you hear me?"

"Right. The driver goes before a judge. He was drinking, so he's going to lose his driver's license."

"The judge does that?"

Skip nodded.

"The law makes it automatic."

"I had a kid on the bus say his cousin was going to get me for telling the police. He got kicked off the bus for a week."

"Ha! Good. They all need to learn a lesson. It's not good to drink and drive. Look at what happened to my Eloise and Libby!"

"You miss them, huh?"

"I've lost a lot," he said, leaning forward. "You did, too. You might have my granddaughter here right now to talk to instead of me."

"I'd like her," Jamella said, as she helped Skip stand. "Can my friend Hannah come again on Saturday?"

He wobbled a bit but settled.

"I'll tell you a secret," he said, not registering Jamella's request for Hannah. "Libby likes you. I see her sometimes. Mostly when I nap."

"Wow, that's cool! Does she talk about heaven and stuff?"

"She doesn't have to, I know she's happy."

"What does she look like? Is she grown-up?"

"I only know she's close, but I don't see her."

The old man placed a hand on the girl's shoulder. Cal whinnied. Ace lazily stood with head down, eyes drooped.

The house, dark from within, looked abandoned, aged, and frail in the early crescent moon's light. He imagined Eloise hanging clothes on a frayed, sagging rope hung from one rusted, crooked steel pole to another with Libby, clothespins in hand, standing by her side. The night air chilled Skip. His eyes watered.

"Am I crazy?" he asked, voice soft.

Jamella wiped at her runny nose.

"No!" she said in the self-assured, direct way that teenagers do.

This helped deflect Skip's next thought of, but why now? Why, after all these years, were Eloise and Libby so close he could feel his heart swell? For Jamella, it was simple. If Skip felt them now, what else mattered? Why waste time parsing the metaphysical, logical, or spiritual reasons?

"Maybe I understand life better now," he said.

Skip patted Jamella's shoulder.

"You got a good head on your shoulders. Don't ever lose your common sense."

"What's that really mean?" she asked with a shrug.

"Hmm, good question."

Skip leaned closer.

"It means you've got a knack for finding the simplest way to solve a problem."

Jamella smiled.

"So, I can see the whole forest, not just the trees. I heard you say that before. I like that one."

Skip straightened.

With his chest out playfully for effect, added, "Guess you can learn something from an old man, after all."

They walked to a fork in the path Jamella took to head home.

She paused.

"In school, everything we learn is important for later, but what about something for now? See ya!" she said, bobbing down the hill, her flashlight splashing upon the rocks, trees, and house below.

"Something for now," the old man mused aloud.

"Very practical, that Miss J," he said to Ace. "But that would make life too easy, huh, boy?"

Skip waited until she entered through the back door before turning. The old man walked home, Ace at his side.

By the kitchen sink stood John, hands and arms busy with a few grocery bags, light from within cast onto the porch.

Skip stopped. It was John's time now, his journey still in full march, while Skip's had all but halted.

He said to Ace, "Looks like we're coming to the last bag-drag, old friend."

He thought of the military, his last day, and Benny, a man who had deserved fairness and honesty, at least, if not justice.

John spoke as Skip hung his jacket by the backdoor, the old man only processing a word or two. With Ace standing faithfully by him, Skip's thoughts were of the two other black Labs that had preceded the current version. All great companions after Eloise had died. On one knee, he wrapped his arms around the dog, its musk smell mild. Ace licked Skip's face, and the old man's eyes welled with gratitude.

"Are you crying?" John asked, wiping his hands on a dishcloth.

He expected his father to make a joke or ignore the question, but Skip said, "These are the best damn dogs..."

"Oh, I thought you were bothered about what I'd just said, thinking that you'd miss me, ha. I will be gone for a few weeks. Setting up a new office is a real pain."

Skip, eyes glazed in thought, had no response so John bent closer and handed a crunchy biscuit to Ace.

"Dad, you okay?" John asked.

"Sure," he said, leaning upon John to stand. "A few weeks. I heard you."

Face to face, John said, "A C.N.A. is going to visit every day at lunch to be sure you've got your meds right and bring something to eat. Then Laura will come by at night."

Skip looked at the prescription bottles lined up on the windowsill, knowing he could not keep them straight.

He was not even sure what they were for but said, "I can take care of myself."

"I know. This is more for my sake than yours. Can you work with that? I met the woman, very nice. You'll like her."

"I'm not going to eat broccoli or kale or that other healthy stuff. What's it called? You know, made out of soy."

They moved into the living room.

"Tofu? Ha! No. She'll ask what you'd like and bring it."

"All right," he said, settling into the faded cloth recliner.

John left his dad seated in front of the television relieved that Skip was willing to go along with a daily visit. He was not happy to leave, but John didn't want to upset his superiors. It was a promotion he had long looked forward to, so he considered it a temporary necessity. John was pleased his dad would have help, especially from Laura, who he grew fonder of every day.

Without giving it a second thought, Laura had agreed, completely easing John's anxiety. Laura would bring the woman on Monday at noon, while John traveled the five hours out-of-state.

Unfortunately, the woman never arrived as planned.

The agency had no one to replace her, apologized to John and then said, "It's very competitive. They are signed right out from under us, usually with a starting bonus."

Luckily, Laura had a temporary solution.

"The woman working here with the painter is a certified home health aide, but she makes more painting with her brother," Laura said. "She's very nice. Her name is Gloria, and she's interested. I'll take her over to meet your dad tomorrow."

John sat at a desk while computer techs and an outside cleaning crew buzzed around him connecting wires and vacuuming carpets. He leaned against a stack of resumes, one hand against his forehead, the other holding a cell phone to his ear.

With a loud exhale he said, "I owe you big time."

"That's what Jamella said."

"Doesn't miss a thing, does she?"

Laura laughed.

"Seriously," John said. "I want to take you out as soon as I'm finished here."

"Oh? No, that's not necessary."

"No," he said, "Like a real date. Me, you and Jamella."

When Laura didn't reply, he asked, "Unless you wouldn't want..."

"That would be nice," Laura said. "Yes, we'd like that."

19

Lucia was nervous and excited to put her training to use. If it went well, she might have a recommendation for the future. She remembered Mrs. Gomez and how finding employment in health care validated the faith the woman had demonstrated in Lucia.

When they arrived, the backdoor to the house was unlocked.

"Let me talk to him first," Laura said, as it appeared Skip might have another visitor.

Skip was alone in the living room, talking aloud.

"I know," Skip said. "Just an accident from a long time ago, but if you want, I'll do it."

Laura wondered if Skip was speaking into his cellphone, but his hands were on his lap.

"Hi," Laura said, rousing the old man. "Brought someone for you to meet."

"I know," he said. "I was just talking about it. Guess it's okay."

"You were?" she said, her eyes scanning the empty room.

Lucia waited in Skip's kitchen rubbing her dry hands. I do need better lotion, she thought, as she waited while Laura spoke to Skip in the living room.

After a bit of explanation, Laura waved for Lucia to join them.

"Frank, this is Gloria."

Lucia stood next to the man who barely made eye contact.

"He's a bit sleepy today," Laura said of Skip seated in the recliner.

He wore a white and blue flannel shirt and black corduroy pants worn a bit at the knees.

Lucia leaned forward, face closer to his, and noticed drool from his mouth.

"Let me get that," she said, dabbing at his lip with a tissue.

"No fancy food," he said, as he absentmindedly looked about at the carpet by his feet.

Laura said, "I know what you like. We'll take care of it. You lose something?"

"What?" Skip said, making eye contact with Lucia.

Lucia leaned back, her ears buzzing, and her mouth dry. Something wasn't right, but what? She was struck by an unsettling familiarity she could not place.

Later in the afternoon, when she and Jesus were painting Laura's living room, Lucia made the connection. Instantly, she felt sick. She ran out the back door and vomited onto a pile of leaves.

Kneeling in the dry ground, her face flushed, sweat on her forehead, she moaned, "God, no!"

Jesus placed a hand on her shaking back.

"It's him," she said. "The husband. From my accident."

"Whoa! Did he say anything to you?"

Lucia wiped her cheeks.

"No. He didn't recognize me."

Helping Lucia to her feet he said, "So, that's good."

"Good! How is that good?" She faced him, cheeks flushed, arms spread wide.

"Shh," he said, grabbing her by the shoulders. "If he doesn't know, or won't ever know, it's a kindness, right?"

She sighed.

"I can't..."

"Let's go inside. Have some water. Think about it more. It's for what, a couple of days?"

In the kitchen Lucia said, "But they might figure out who I am. I need a *new* start."

As she sipped from a Thermos, Jesus said, "You might be known for what happened, but how do you want to be remembered?"

Lucia leaned against the sink.

"I just didn't expect it to happen so soon—or this way—that my past would come back like *boom*, in my face."

Outside, Laura arrived a minute before the school bus. She greeted Jamella when the girl hopped off the bus, and Lucia felt a pang of pity. Would Lucia ever have a family or a normal life? I have to tell the woman," Lucia said, wiping her face by the window's reflection. "It's only right."

"Yes," Jesus said. "Let her decide. Do you want me to wait with you?"

"No. You can pack up."

Lucia heard their voices, light, pleasant, and happy, then Jamella's footsteps on the stairs to her room.

Laura walked into the kitchen and smiled.

"Are you still okay with helping Skip?"

Lucia nodded.

"There's something you should know. I was in a car accident."

Lucia paused, eyes down.

"His wife and granddaughter both died."

"Oh my...it was you?" Laura said, taking a seat at the table. "How awful! I mean, for both of you."

Lucia shuddered, her voice caught in her throat. The room was quiet and closed around Lucia like a cell.

Finally, she said, "I don't know if I should do it."

"Here," Laura said, pushing a chair to her, "sit. I know what happened. Jamella found it on-line."

Lucia's eyes watered.

"Things last on-line forever."

"They do. But do you want to try again tomorrow? Skip might not remember you. In the meantime, I can call the agency to see if someone else can take over."

"My brother says it can be an act of kindness."

Laura's face brightened.

"Absolutely! It would really help if you could stay on for a day or two. Let's see what happens tomorrow. I'll go with you. If he doesn't remember, it'll be a good thing. Might even make you feel better."

The idea of another day or two went over better as she spoke to Andres that night while at a diner. They were both hungry and tired. Lucia felt a bit dizzy and weak.

"Here," Andres said, sliding a handful of sweet potato fries onto her plate, "you'll like these."

Lucia smiled.

"Thanks. Did I make too big a deal about today? It was a surprise."

"Maybe you don't like surprises," Andres said, counting out twenty-one dollars. "Although some are better than others, like you and me becoming friends. I didn't think your brother would let me get near you because of my situation back home."

Lucia rose from the red vinyl bench seat.

"That's probably why he did. Thought you'd be safe."

Andres winked.

"If he only knew."

She scoffed.

"There's nothing to know. Yet."

Lucia had given thought to their relationship becoming intimate, but there would be rules first, she thought as they drove to her apartment. It would be a benefit of their friendship, not love, she knew. She didn't want to become romantically involved with a married man. Lucia did give thought to his family in Guatemala and while it bothered her to betray another woman, she had rationalized that she and Andres were lonely, and the intimacy would be temporary and non-committal. She refused to be a homewrecker or the other woman. Still, she found herself watching his backside when he walked and liked how he groomed a short beard.

She knew sex was inevitable and imagined a romantic outing with candle light, cloth table coverings, and waiters graciously joking with them as if they were newly wed. These thoughts lingered with her as they folded freshly cleaned laundry in the kitchen of her apartment.

"Jesus will be happy," Andres said. "This is the cleanest these coveralls have been in a long while."

At the table, they stood across from each other, sorting their work clothes and placing them in respective piles. When their fingers touched, she grabbed Andres' hand. Their physical attraction sparked, and Lucia felt the pull of need, of a longing so strong, her hand trembled.

"It's okay," he said, holding her close.

The warmth of their lips and tongues summoned an energy Lucia did not know she had, and she let herself go. He lifted Lucia into his arms, her knee knocking against the table as he carried her to the bedroom.

She clung to him as they lay on the bed, hands sliding under his shirt. Andres' back was lean, warm, and soft. The longing Lucia felt was as much sexual as was the need to be held and feel loved. The image of her father, sweaty and tired at the end of his workday, smiling at Lucia from the driveway popped into her mind. *Loved.* And she knew the moment was wrong. As he caressed her thighs, she pulled his hands away.

"No," she whispered, her hands within his. "No."

"Did I do..." he began, voice trailing off.

Her deep, glassy eyes were a mix of passion and sadness. Lucia forced a thin smile.

"I understand," he said, moving close to her side.

Andres moved a wisp of hair from her face and tucked it behind her ear. He held Lucia, feeling her deep sigh.

"I have to be better," she said, as she wiped her eyes. "So much was done for me."

Andres, his head against Lucia's back, thought of his wife and son and said nothing. She was right, he knew, as the passion faded.

While he was in the bathroom, Lucia covered herself with a sheet. Fluffing the pillow, she placed it against the headboard to rest her head and shoulders. Water splashed with the squeak of a faucet handle, and she sighed contentedly. All these years of waiting, wondering, and imagining what it would be like to share a bed with a man, and it was already over. Another prison "can't wait to" *almost* ticked off the list. It had not happened as romantically she had dreamed it would, but Andres was a gentleman, and she was happy not to have gone too far. A sense of new-found dignity squared her head and shoulders, and she was relieved.

Andres returned and sat at the edge of the bed.

Buttoning his shirt he asked, "Are we okay?"

Lucia extended her hand to him.

"As long as we don't make this a habit."

"Yes," he said, releasing her hand. "You stopped in time. Still," he said, with a sly smile, "it was nice, yes?"

She smiled.

"It was wonderful, but we have to stay friends, right?"

"Right," he said, standing. "I know."

Later, after Andres left, Lucia lingered in the shower, letting warm water cascade over her hair and shoulders until the hot water ran low. She toweled off, then sat in the darkness of the kitchen looking into the backyard. She knew it couldn't happen again. One time was a mistake, two times was deliberate, and her thoughts went to Andre's wife and son. *No, not again.*

"I have to be better," she said, lightly rapping a knuckle on the table.

Lucia sipped from a tumbler filled with cold water, ice, and a slice of lime. Sex with Andre was not the worst mistake she had ever made. The accident was, and making amends by helping the old man softened her guilt.

I can do this, she thought. *I will help him.*

20

Jamella's problems did not end with Mike's bus suspension. Upon return from school on Monday, Jamella and Hannah found a crowd of students standing in front of her locker, laughing and talking loudly.

When the two girls approached, the kids quieted, eyes wide with expectation. They stood aside to reveal a picture of a chimpanzee sitting on a tree branch with the word, "snitch" written across the animal's chest.

Jamella froze, mouth open, eyes watering, but Hannah was decisive. She tore the taped picture from the locker.

Angrily crumbling it into a ball, she said, "So not funny!" and the expected drama dissipated.

Jamella, with head down, fought tears as she twisted the combination lock. Once open, she tucked her head inside and sobbed once, softly. Her face, neck, and back were aflame with humiliation. She had been teased in the past, but never before a whole grade of her peers. She was the bullseye and their scorn the arrow. Jamella now knew the depth of their dislike for her. She took a deep breath.

"Let's go," Hannah said, slamming her locker door shut. "Only a total loser would do that," she said loudly for the benefit of those standing in the hall.

For the rest of the day, Jamella's cheeks burned whenever someone laughed or stared, so she avoided eye contact.

Later, on the bus ride home she said to Hannah, "Thanks for helping me."

Jamella's throat filled with emotion.

"You're welcome," she said, turning a page in a paperback. "Don't let it bother you."

Jamella thought of her first day taking the bus and how only Hannah had made eye contact with Jamella, then slid over so the new girl would have a seat.

"Why did you let me sit with you here on that first day?"

Without looking up, she said, "I saw this," Hannah said, tapping a finger on Jamella's sketchpad. "I didn't think you'd talk much if you liked to draw. And those kids in the back wouldn't have left you alone so..."

Jamella paused, watching as the blond haired, blue-eyed girl read. Jamella had made friends before, but only out of necessity, either to keep a secret or because sticking together kept them from being bullied or stolen from. She opened her pad and with a new, sharp pencil, drew Hannah as she sat reading, the afternoon light bright around her. Hannah was her friend for no other reason than she had wanted a quiet seatmate. Sometimes, friendship could just be that easy.

Without Mike to egg them on, the boys in the back were quiet, and Jamella relaxed. Having Hannah by her side was like having her butterfly Lucy, always quiet, always with her. She thought of Jenny, her first friend, who stole Hershey Kisses from a convenience store and shared them with Jamella as they walked home from grammar school. Eddie, who was older, looked out for Jamella because she hid his e-cigarettes in her school bag.

Pretty Hannah, envied by both boys and girls and who could have all the friends she wanted, chose one, Jamella. As Jamella drew, she sensed the quiet Hannah craved also came tinged with sadness.

Jamella put the pencil down and rested the back of her head against the cool vinyl bench seat. She realized everyone, even the beautiful Hannah, could be as Jamella was, both happy and sad. Happy for her life now, but sad for those she had left behind. Luckily, an afternoon visit with Cal and Ace would perk Jamella up.

She was surprised to see Skip standing with Gloria in the barn.

"Tough day, J?" Skip asked of the girl, who walked with shoulders drooped.

"You look tired," Gloria said.

"Why are you here?" Jamella asked.

"I'm going to help Mister Skip for a few days while John's away."

Skip sat on a hay bale and rubbed Ace's ears. Jamella went to the horse with a brush and Lucia moved to her. "So," she asked, "tell me about school. What's your favorite subject?"

"I don't like school," she said, quietly. "Kids are mean, except for my friend."

Jamella then told Lucia about the sign on her locker.

"That's hateful," Lucia said, causing Jamella to sigh and drop her head onto Cal's flank.

Tears formed in the girl's eyes.

"It hurts, but tomorrow you'll be better. The more they hate, the stronger they make us."

"Kids were mean to you?"

Lucia put a hand on Jamella's shoulder.

"Oh, yes. And I was...mean, too. Hate's an easy club to belong to, but it's awful."

"It's because you're different," Skip said. "It's always been a problem."

"Did they ever apologize for ruining the sign?" Gloria asked.

Skip scoffed.

"Nah."

They finished in the barn and Jamella headed for home. Lucia and Skip waited as she navigated the slope, arms out, moving confidently. When she reached the back door, the couple turned, Lucia walking alongside Skip, who took small steps.

Lucia didn't grab his arm, as he did not like a fuss, but she was alert for a stumble. He was tipped forward, head down, shuffling rather than lifting his feet, which worried her. Skip was diagnosed with Lewy Body Dementia, which affected his balance and caused occasional delusions. Lucia made sure he took his meds and ate the burger, vanilla shake and fries she had brought for him.

"You got to eat better," she said, as he sipped on a straw.

"But I'm full," he said, pushing the half-eaten burger away.

"Not more," she said, "healthy food," but he didn't respond. "Tomorrow, you show me how to do laundry. You've worn the same clothes for two days now. Will be good to change."

She left him seated in the recliner to watch television.

Jesus drove her home. He was shaved, showered, and neatly dressed. He wore an open collared blue shirt with black pants.

"Got a date," Jesus said with a smile. "You can't be the only one to have fun."

When she arrived the following day, Skip was talking loudly in the kitchen, and she wondered if Laura had stopped in to see him. When she heard only his voice, Lucia knocked and waited. Skip came and opened the door. His eyes were clouded with misunderstanding.

"Remember me?" she asked, watching as his eyes searched her face. "I came yesterday with Miss Laura. Did I interrupt anything?"

Skip shook his head.

"Just talking with my wife. She forgives you."

"Oh?" Lucia croaked, her throat tight. "For, umm, what?"

Skip handed a small chew treat to Ace, the dog waiting patiently at his side.

With a smirk he said, "For being late."

Lucia exhaled.

"Ah, full of jokes, huh? Guess you're feeling good today."

Skip made two fists.

"I feel great every day!"

Lucia placed half-pound packets of ham, American cheese, and turkey in the refrigerator.

"I have a surprise. A homemade bean burrito lightly seasoned so you won't have heartburn."

"Heartburn? What kind of food is that?"

"The tasty and filling kind," she said, placing the wrap in front of him.

He sniffed at it.

"Ah, I don't think Ace would eat this."

Lucia scoffed.

"You'll like it, trust me."

Skip paused, thinking. The words, "trust me," hanging between them.

Finally, Skip took a small bite.

"See," she said, "just hamburger, corn, avocado and cheese."

"You're lucky I'm hungry," Skip said, holding the wrap with both hands.

"Sabelotodo," she said with a smile. "Means smart ass. That's you."

"Sounds nice when you say it."

Lucia cleaned the kitchen counters and laid out Skip's meds while he sat in the living room reading a crumpled newspaper. She took note of what little he had left for milk, dog food, and of the expired items—vitamins, aspirin, and cough syrup—in his kitchen and medicine cabinets and threw them into the trash. With a straw broom, she knocked cobwebs from the ceiling and swept the floor.

When finished, she called, "Mister Skip, let's do the laundry."

"Oh," he said eyes on a crossword puzzle. "My wife does that."

Lucia, now by Skip's side said, "Come, show me."

She grabbed his arm and helped him to his feet. Lucia let Skip lead her down the creaking wood of the basement stairs, her fingers lightly upon his belt. The washer and dryer sat together behind the stairs and underneath a wispy netting of spider webs. An old, misshapen laundry basket half-filled with handkerchiefs, socks, towels and underwear awaited. Lucia was not surprised there were no clothes to wash, since he was in the habit of wearing the same faded clothes daily. Skip smelled, too, of barn and talcum, and she wondered how often he showered.

Skip put a cup of detergent into the washer barrel, then Lucia dumped the clothes into it. She pressed the normal cycle button and listened as water sputtered and hissed while filling the tub. "What's in those?" Lucia asked of the cardboard tubes racked from floor to ceiling against the stone foundation's back wall.

Skip squinted.

"Hmm."

He took a few steps around some used paint cans and over a long-empty, flat, bird seed bag covered with mice scat to pull one cylinder from the rest.

"These are mechanical shop drawings. I made copies of them because the originals were for work. Gave me something to do after Eloise, you know?"

Lucia sighed.

"Oh, yes, your wife. Sorry for your loss," she said, rubbing her hands.

He replaced the cardboard tube.

"What else can you say, right?"

"Jamella would like these. Has she seen some of them?"

Skip shrugged, and waited for Lucia to speak. He looked closely at her, like he had found something and wondered what it was.

Lucia added, "I am really, really sorry for what happened."

The old man stood in the glare of the ceiling bulb, his eyes fixed on hers.

The musty air caught in Lucia's throat and the need to be honest was overwhelming.

"Do you know my name?" she asked. "I mean, do you know who I am?"

"I do. You're the bad driver."

Skip sat on a rusty stool by the dryer and extended his legs. Folding his hands onto his lap, he said nothing more.

Lucia looked into his pale, flat eyes and understood he wasn't kidding.

"You knew all along?"

"Yup."

Lucia felt her chest sink.

"I didn't mean to trick you. I'm sorry if—"

"Are you going to wash this stuff?"

"You want me to stay?"

"At least until the wash is done," he said, plainly.

He extended his bony hand, and she took it, expecting to help Skip stand.

Instead, he held her fingers within his and added, "You never meant any harm. A random accident in a messy world, and it was our turn to get bit. If I stood on top of the mistakes I've made, I could shake God's hand."

The weight of his words made Lucia kneel at his feet. Skip placed a hand on her hair and waited while she cried. The washing machine sloshed and vibrated.

Finally, Skip said, "Okay, let's go."

"Thank you. Your words mean so much."

"Ah, that wasn't me. It was something Eloise would say."

Skip offered a handkerchief.

"Go ahead, take it. It's clean."

Lucia wiped her eyes and nose.

Skip lifted the washer lid.

"Throw it in here, unless you need to *slobber* some more."

"Ha. You like being a smart ass, huh?"

"Pays the bills."

Even though her emotions were spent, she laughed.

"So, you quit your day job to tell corny jokes? How's that working for you?"

Skip, standing by the bottom of the staircase, crinkled his eyes.

"Who's the wise ass now?"

21

John spoke to Laura on the Wednesday of Lucia's first week of caring for Skip. Laura assured him it was going well.

"Your dad gives her the business, but she gives it right back."

"He likes that. You should've heard him and my mom. Honestly, like the Costanzas on *Seinfeld*, just not as mean. But, listen, I appreciate how you've handled this, and I haven't forgotten about our dinner date with Jamella, as soon as I'm back in a couple of weeks."

Laura stood in the kitchen, cell phone tucked under her neck wiping dishes, while Jamella put on her sneakers.

"I haven't forgotten."

"Just so you know," John said, "I, um, would like it to be a *family* date. I mean, I've been thinking about you two a lot, and I'd like to see if we could be closer. Is that okay?"

Laura smiled.

"Yes, we're looking forward to it, still."

"Hmm, sorry, been a bit busy. I might as well be open about my intentions with both of you, right?"

Jamella took a cookie from a white ceramic jar and chewed as her mother spoke.

With a tease Laura said, "So you like both of us, huh?" taking the girl's attention away from the vanilla crème wafers.

"Was that John?" Jamella asked, after Laura said goodbye.

"Yes. I teased John about liking us because he's so happy to have our help."

"He likes you more than me, but that's good," she said, putting an empty glass of milk into the dishwasher. "If you marry John, do I have to call him dad?"

Laura laughed.

"Oh, my. Who says that's even going to happen?"

Jamella grabbed her jacket.

"Because you like each other. Pretty obvious."

"I do, but that doesn't mean—"

"I'm okay with it. Being a family would be awesome," Jamella said, going outside through the back door.

Jamella had been in four different foster homes before the adoption. Laura never asked Jamella how it felt to bounce around or be loved as a member of a family. The social worker explained that children respond differently to moving. Some become outgoing to pursue friendship and comfort, while others remain somewhat withdrawn finding solace in themselves.

"Jamella's an interesting case," the male who handled her case file said. "She's quiet until she's comfortable, then there's no filter, *at all*. Jamella's a sweet kid, talented, and well-behaved. Like most, all she wants is stability, to be a part of a family."

Laura had never asked Jamella much of her past, and the girl offered little when asked, so Laura assumed all had gone reasonably well under the circumstances. Jamella was housed, fed, educated, and kept healthy in the foster system, but was that enough?

With the newness that came with Jamella's adoption, Laura had never wondered what it was like to have no place to call home. Her only inkling came when she had broken from her fiancé and resolved to continue without the support of family—too embarrassed by the failure to marry to spend time with them—and it was a lonely time.

Work kept her busy, but an empty studio apartment is not much more than a motel room upgrade, no matter how many plants or cats await. Like water leaking from a pail, the newness of being on her own evaporated, and Laura adjusted. She became independent in ways Jamella had to develop as well, but was that the best way for a young child, or budding teen, to grow?

Only after having Jamella did Laura see the nuances that shape children into who they will later become, and so she worried and wondered about what was right and wrong about her parenting. Who would have thought a grumpy old man sitting in a rundown barn would have a son for Laura, or a horse her daughter adored?

She watched as the girl walked the hill to the barn, Laura's face shining on the window.

To her likeness she said, "Maybe this is finally it."

She looked at the circles under her eyes and thought maybe a change of makeup... Could John finally be the one? She lay in bed later, hopeful. Her happiness, though, would be short-lived.

In the morning, Jamella noticed white paint splashed against the front of the house and porch, as it cast the sun's light brightly into the parlor.

"What in the world?" Laura said, a can of empty paint lying on its side at the bottom step, the lid nearby.

"Maybe our painters left it," she said, unsure.

She phoned Jesus, who later arrived as Sergeant Wilson took a statement.

"Friday night drinking," he said, with a shake of his head. "Probably a prank but let me look around."

Jesus observed the swath of white splashed against the beige vinyl siding and wood porch decking.

"Luckily, it's water based," he said, "and easy to clean up."

Softly, he added, "This isn't good, though."

The sergeant returned from a walk around the property. He pushed his cap back.

"Looks like someone came up the walkway, splashed the paint and drove away. No footprints, so that's good. They didn't case the place. Get a quote for the damage and submit it with my report to your insurance company."

Wilson tore the report from a copy pad.

"You might want to get a security camera. Easy to do-it-yourself now. I'll ask around. Again, hopefully, just a prank."

"I can give you a quote for labor," Jesus said. "No paint needed."

As Wilson drove off, Laura said, "What do you know about security cameras?"

"I'll get one for you, fairly cheap. You'll be alerted if someone's around."

Laura shuddered.

"Never expected this. I feel . . . *targeted.*"

"Let's hope not," Jesus said. "Let me get a pair of coveralls and I'll clean this up quick."

"Do you have two pairs? If this is because of who I picked to paint my house, then I'm not giving them the satisfaction of letting you clean this alone," Laura said with a flash of anger in her eyes. "Jamella and I will help."

Using warm water gently misted upon the vinyl siding along with the use of soft brushes soaked in dishwashing soap, the paint slowly loosened and fell into puddles on the deck. Jamella worked patiently, but Laura grew angrier with each stroke of the soft brush against the decking. By noon, the paint was gone, but the clean deck and wall stood out.

"I have to bring my sister next door," Jesus said, standing by the van. "But Monday, I'll wash the rest of the front so it will all be clean and blend in."

Laura and Jamella sat side by side upon the top porch step and waved to Jesus as he drove away.

"Gosh, we're lucky to have both of them, huh?" Laura said. "But it sure ticks me off that someone would be so hateful."

Jamella shrugged.

"Hate makes them strong."

"It does," Laura said, flashing back to Jesus' comment about minorities working in her neighborhood. "You deal with more than I know, too. How can I help?"

Jamella shrugged.

"It's like Gloria says, 'Just be me'".

Laura wrapped an arm around Jamella's shoulders. "When did she tell you that?"

"Yesterday. We were just talking. She understands."

Laura nodded, grateful Jamella could relate to Gloria. Skin color was the last thing on Laura's mind since the adoption. So much had to be done to bring Jamella into Laura's home—enrolling in school, food, clothing, maintaining Laura's business, and learning to be comfortable around each other—had preoccupied Laura.

Finally, she said, "Good advice, but let's talk when something upsets you, how's that?"

Jamella, picking at flakes of white paint on her fingernails said, "This wasn't about the painters. It's about me. They're mad because I called the police when the sign got smashed. I'm a snitch."

Laura leaned forward.

"No, you're not. And who's they?"

"Nobody," Jamella said, standing. "Just some stupid kids. One was suspended for a week."

146

"Good. We're going to ramp up security here. Jesus will install some security cameras for us. Wish I could do the same for you at school."

Jamella rolled her eyes.

"You mean like a body cam?"

Laura smiled.

"I wonder if Jesus can get one of those."

"No thanks!" Jamella said, feigning frustration. "I know you would, too."

Later, as they stood at the kitchen sink scrubbing their hands under warm water, Jamella asked, "You're not mad that I tell Gloria stuff, are you?"

"No, and I understand why. When I brought you here, I didn't think about this," she said, touching a white finger to Jamella's dark brown hand, "but you're happy here, right?"

Jamella nodded.

"It's like she's my aunt, almost."

"That's nice," Laura said, wrapping her arm around the girl's thin shoulders, and thinking it would be good to talk to Gloria. With nursing aides unavailable, she had to tell John soon about the woman caring for his dad. It had been almost a week, and with each passing day, Laura felt guilty about not telling John. A different aide was unlikely, so before she called John, she sat with Gloria.

While Jamella went to the barn, Laura met with Gloria in Skip's kitchen. A line of seven pill bottles with their caps off sat on the counter.

"That's handy," Laura said of the three weekly pill organizers, their tops open waiting for white, pink, and blue tablets to be added for each of the seven days.

"Yes, one for morning, noon, and night," Lucia said with a chuckle. "It was hard for me to remember, so I bought these to help."

She wore a blue nurse's smock, white sneakers, loose fitting pants, blue latex gloves, and had her black, straight hair tied in a ponytail. Despite wearing no makeup, her cheeks glistened, and her eyes shone.

"You're enjoying this, huh?" Laura asked.

"Glad someone is," Skip said with a smirk.

He stood in the living room doorway, his face cleanly shaven.

"All right, handsome, quit flirting," Lucia said, handing him a pill. "Here, go slow. Only three to take now."

Skip took one at a time with sips of water.

"Tip your head back a bit," Lucia said, pushing gently on his wrinkled forehead.

She asked Laura, "What brings you by? No more paint troubles, I hope."

"Thank God, no. You're okay with staying on two more weeks?"

"Hmm. This guy's not easy."

"Bull," Skip said, taking a seat at the table. "I should get something extra for all the abuse I'm taking."

The women laughed.

"Poor you," Lucia said.

"We do have one real problem," Laura said, as she slipped a blue wool jacket off her shoulders. "John still doesn't know about this. We should tell him."

Lucia leaned against the counter.

She sighed, "Okay, how?"

Laura waved an iPhone.

"Facetime. I did think about going out to meet him, but it's too far."

"Ah, why?" Skip said. "It's none of his business."

"Have you ever done this?" Laura asked Skip. "You can see someone when you're talking. Like the old 'Dick Tracy' comics."

With a look of disapproval, he shook his head.

"Never done it, or don't like the idea?" Laura asked.

"Both," Skip said. "He won't like knowing, so why tell him?"

Laura shrugged.

"What if he came home unexpectedly?"

"That would be worse," Lucia said.

Skip blew air through his lips.

"Suit yourself."

John answered the second ring.

"This is a nice surprise, I hope."

"Got your dad and Gloria here," she said, turning the phone to Skip, who squinted at the screen.

"Hey, Dad. Look at you, mister tech savvy. Don't tell me you want a smartphone."

"A what?"

"Ha! Never mind. You're looking good. Guess Gloria's doing a great job. Thank you, Gloria."

Gloria's chest sunk and she turned her face from the table. Eyes dull, her happiness gone, she put a hand on the counter top to steady herself.

"Look, Son, here's the deal. I like her, so she's not going anywhere, and—"

"Gloria? Great. I won't bother the agency. Let me talk to her."

"She's the one from the accident."

"What accident?"

"The wrong way driver."

"What? Oh, Dad," John scoffed. "Come on."

Skip handed the phone to Laura.

"What's he saying?"

Laura took a deep breath.

"I'm sorry, John. None of us knew."

"I did," Skip said loudly, "and it's okay."

"What? Are you kidding me? If this is a joke, it's as funny as cancer!"

The kitchen quieted.

Finally, John said, "What the...? I want her out, Dad."

"She's staying put. Your mother's orders."

"Mom? Dad, she's not here anymore! That's the whole freaking problem! Can you even trust her?"

"I do," Skip said with confidence. "Don't you worry about that."

"Laura, why didn't you tell me?" John said, with a sudden, stinging pain exploding between his eyes.

"She's telling you now," Skip said. "You got to get over it. Stop walking a crooked line."

"Get over it! Are you serious? Unbelievable. And here I am thinking everything's good."

John's anger spread through him like fire.

"Damn!"

The phone went dark.

Laura sighed.

"He'll probably try the agency again."

Lucia nodded.

"I should go."

"Your work isn't done," Skip said.

Tapping his chest, he added, "I decide who helps me."

Tears came to Lucia's eyes.

Laura said, "I'll call him after he's calmed down. You've done well. Why change anything now?"

Lucia nodded.

"Thank you," she said, throat thick with emotion.

"All right, enough of this," Skip said. "Let's get to the barn."

They each took a side and walked with the old man, who took his usual short, shuffling steps.

"Where have you all been?" Jamella asked, just as a text appeared on Laura's phone.

The girl stood by Cal, brush in hand.

The text read, "Do you understand how awful this is? How did you let it happen?"

Laura responded, "It just did, sorry. I'll call later."

"Don't bother!"

Laura's forehead reddened. No good deed goes unpunished, she thought, so she decided not to reply. Skip was happy, and Gloria was in place. John's anger was expected, and not something Laura could fix. Maybe time would.

When Jesus arrived to take Lucia home, she quietly asked Laura, "Should I come tomorrow?"

"Yes."

"Even though, the son–"

"He's not the patient," Laura said, forcing a smile. "It'll be okay."

22

After leaving the office, John stopped at a liquor store and bought a bottle of gin.

"So, I'm back to like nothing's changed," he said, when he entered the motel room.

He placed his keys on the nightstand.

Slamming his jacket down on the bed, he swore, "Screw it!"

Trapped by the past and by the inability to find someone to care for his dad, he grew angrier as he sat in the faded and lumpy armchair, his dirty clothes piled on the carpet near the heater.

"What a life," he said, twisting the cap off the bottle.

He sniffed the alcohol, remembering its familiar ting. After a swig, he capped the gin and set it upon the floor. He rested his head against the back of the chair. The intensity of the day had taken the life out of him, so he dozed.

John woke later to the sound of a loud muffler and a booming car radio thumping from outside. The room was partially dark, the only light filtering in from the lamps in the parking lot. He sniffed his clothes and realized he had nothing clean to wear. He remembered his dad's admonition to, "stop walking a crooked line." More like walking in circles, he thought, grabbing for the bottle of gin.

He picked up the dirty clothes, grabbed his room key and then walked to the motel's laundry room. There, he watched the tumble of soapy water while he sipped gin. With each turn, a different item of clothing sloshed against the front loader glass, and he found himself waiting for the same piece to return, curious as to whether there was a pattern to the tumbling, but it was entirely random. Later, he would stack his clothes on a chair and fall asleep, his mind and heart empty.

He woke to his alarm with a sore head and a churning stomach. He slurped water from the bathroom faucet, ate a breakfast bar, and wished he could go back to sleep. He swallowed four aspirin, opened his laptop, and decided to ignore a list of emails. They could wait until he was at the office.

When ready, he opened the motel room door against the heavy push of fresh, cool air. The sun shone brightly, so he turned his head back toward his dreary room with the bottle of gin sitting on the nightstand.

I have no life, he thought, locking the door.

Sitting in the car, he sighed. If that's what the stubborn S.O.B. wants, he can have it. Still, the situation with Lucia didn't sit well with him. He called his partner at work to say he had a family emergency, then began the five-hour drive home.

On the way, John called two home health care agencies.

One call ended with, "If you find one, you're lucky."

Discouraged, he stopped at a donut shop to use the men's room. He left with a coffee and muffin and questioned his decision to go to Skip's.

Admittedly, the reality of having Lucia care for his dad had sunk in deeper with each passing mile, but there was a point to be made. She could not just ruin someone's life and act as if it never happened. If nothing else, he would let Lucia know that while his failing father may believe it was okay, John knew better. He was on to her, and being kind to Skip was *not* going to absolve her of the pain she had caused. Lucia had a debt to pay, and John was going to remind her of it so even after her three weeks were finished. She would remember the pain, hurt, and suffering she had caused.

"Served her time my ass," he said, stopping the car in Skip's driveway.

John entered through the back door and ignored Ace's tail-wagging greeting. The kitchen and living room were empty, but he heard voices from the second floor bath. He quietly climbed each step gently, listening, wondering what crazy ideas she was putting into Skip's head.

"There," Lucia said, as she combed Skip's hair.

His face was freshly shaved, and he wore a blue cotton shirt, not the usual checkered flannel.

"You're a new man, today."

She helped him from the chair.

"Okay," she said, "let's get to the kitchen. Got meds to take."

Raising her eyes, she saw John's shadow in the hall.

"Oh!" she said, with a jump, squeezing Skip's forearm.

"Oww," the old man said, tugging his arm away.

He followed Lucia's eyes to John.

"No, no. Don't want any trouble today, Son."

"It is you! I can't believe it," he said to Lucia. "You've got some freaking nerve."

Skip stepped in front of her.

"What are you doing here?"

"Had to see it for myself," he said with a shake of his head. "The same woman who killed my mother and daughter standing in our house. No shame, huh?"

"It's *my* house," Skip said, straightening to his full height.

"Helping yourself to the jewelry?" John sneered. "Maybe some bills from his wallet? Dad, when was the last time you checked your credit card statement?"

"What the hell are you talking about?" Skip said, seemingly confused. "I only use cash."

"No kidding. Any missing?"

Lucia's anger found its voice.

"I'm not a thief. See for yourself."

John's eyes shining, face red, said, "I want you out of here. Now!"

"No!" the old man yelled.

"Dad. What do you even know about her? Did you check her background? Oh, right, she was in *jail*. Perfect person to trust in our house, Dad, *our* house. Did you forget I grew up here? Or maybe you forgot those years without mom, without Libby. My Libby!"

Placing hands onto his head, John swallowed hard.

"Oh, god...," he said, voice choked, weak.

"Now listen," Skip said, stepping forward.

"He's right," Lucia said, calmly. "I should go."

Skip, arms shaking, spittle on his chin, said, "She's staying, and you can either leave or get used to it."

"Then I'm leaving," John said, raising a finger to point at Lucia. "Anything happens to him...*anything!* And never mind the police, I'll get you. I swear."

"I'll be fine," Skip said, his lips curled into a smile.

"Sure, like mom and Libby were until this drunk dipshit came along. Blasting the radio, back seat full of empty beer cans..."

"I'm not that person anymore," Lucia said, looking squarely into John's dark-circled eyes.

"Good. Did enough damage, huh? Ruined plenty of lives."

"Yes. Including my own."

"I don't care about yours. You *deserve* to suffer. But, gee, you're free now, right? Hey, do you see my mom when you're here? Chit chat a bit? No, I didn't think so."

"That's enough," Skip said.

He raised his arms to push past John, but his face turned white, and he dropped to one knee.

Lucia checked his pulse, fingers to his neck.

"Your heart is racing. Have you had anything to drink today besides coffee?"

When Skip didn't respond, she said to John, "There's a cup on the bathroom sink."

Lucia helped Skip sit on the floor with his back against the wall.

John brought water, and Lucia placed it to Skip's mouth.

"Let's go. Drink."

John bent at the waist, rubbed his face and eyes.

"There's Gatorade in the refrigerator," Lucia said. "Let's get him downstairs. You go first."

Lucia positioned Skip against John's back and wrapped the old man's arms around John's waist. She then leaned lightly onto Skip, and they went down the stairs slowly, bodies pressed together. They walked with steps gently coordinated, feet carefully placed. At the landing, John took Skip and sat him in the recliner. Lucia brought the drink and offered it to John.

"Here," she said.

John took the cap from the plastic bottle, as Lucia turned to leave.

"Wait," John said. "He wants you."

Lucia shook her head no.

Reaching for her jacket, John said, "He's worse than I thought. Damn, I can't believe this... I need you to stay. *All day.*"

"When did you get here?" the old man said, between sips. "Where's Gloria?"

"I'm here," she said, moving into Skip's line of sight.

Skip winked.

"She's good to me. We're a team."

"I can see that," John said, his voice barely a whisper.

While Lucia sat with Skip, John went to the kitchen window and looked out at Cal, as the horse nibbled grass by the back fence. The sky was blue and deep for miles, and trees held new buds in the warm spring air.

John sighed. Idyllic yet maddeningly ironic, he was trapped by fate. Was he to be punished forever for wanting to stay at the golf course and have another drink? To sleep in an hour longer? His stomach churned so he filled a glass with water and drank. Head still sore from too much gin, John sat at the table.

The fruit bowl, which usually collected car keys and junk mail, now held bananas, red apples, and oranges as it had when Eloise was alive. As opposed to the scents of dog and old shoes, the room smelled bleachy-clean and the counters and wood floor shone.

Lucia, standing in the archway of the living room said to John, "I didn't know it was your dad. It was only going to be for a day or two. I didn't mean to bring trouble."

"But trouble follows you," he said, with his back to her.

When Lucia didn't reply, his anger calmed, replaced by overwhelming feelings of uselessness and defeat. It was pointless to fight, to be angry, or to curse their fates. The cosmic joke was on him.

John stood.

Without looking at her he said, "Stay as long as he wants you to."

Stopping at the end of Skip's driveway, John looked at the crushed No Littering sign, flattened and covered with tire tracks. Where the posts had broken, sharp edges stood. Splattered yet prickly, its footprint remained, along with the ruts made by spinning tires caught by the splintered posts. Even as it was being crushed, the sign had managed still to fight.

Heated by the sun, the car's interior was hot. The lack of fresh air made John's chest tighten and his breathing quicken until he gasped for air. He opened the driver's side door and sat sideways, his feet on the blacktop. Within a minute, the back of his shirt was stained with sweat. He knew from his running days in high school to breathe slowly and deeply though his mouth, but it was hard. John fought with his chest to slow down. Air whistled in and out through pursed lips.

Damn, it was harder to regulate than he remembered.

John squeezed his eyes shut to focus. Don't panic, he reminded himself. Slower, deeper, that's it. With his arms locked, and hands on knees, he kept on for a few minutes until he regained control. The anxiety left John with a terrible headache, one much worse than what the gin had. He sat back in the car, head against the seat rest, vowing never to touch another drop.

Once at the motel, he poured the alcohol down the sink drain, all the time knowing it was more than booze that had caused him to hyperventilate. It was the sense of being trapped, the same feeling he lived with long after Libby had died, which had snagged him again.

The first had happened when he imagined Libby inside a closed coffin, the second when he spotted Carol arm-in-arm with another man as she left a movie theater.

Now, it was knowing he had no choice but to leave Skip in Lucia's care, causing the latest episode.

He took a long, hot shower and decided to let go, finally, of what was out of his control. With a towel around his waist, he laid on the bed, closed his eyes and slept. Chilled, he awoke after midnight, the parking lot unusually quiet. He slid under the sheets, wishing for no dreams.

23

Friday afternoon, Jamella was excited for the weekend. Hannah would spend Saturday with her and with Cal, Ace, Gloria, and Skip, who promised to let her take Cal for a walk on the trails. She stood by the crest of the hill, a shiny black Cadillac parked by the house having caught her attention. Cal was at the other end of the field, his tail casually swishing, and standing in the shade of the pines lined along the wood fence.

An older man, wearing a blue suit, white shirt and red tie, stomped away from the porch, his cheeks red. He caught sight of Jamella and shook his head. When he drove off, the car's tires spun and reminded Jamella of the ruined littering sign.

The visitor, a member of the town council and uncle of the young man, Tyler, who destroyed the sign, asked Skip to drop the vandalism charge so that it wouldn't negatively affect Tyler's acceptance to prep school.

"He's a hell of a skater and goal scorer. This is a chance to earn a free ride, imagine, a free ride!" the man pleaded. "His parents don't have much. You'd give him a better chance at getting in. Really, he's a good kid, like a son to me."

At this, Skip standing with arms folded by the kitchen table, raised a hand to his forehead and covered his eyes.

After a moment, he asked, "And whose truck was he driving?"

The man's eyes widened.

With some hesitation, he said, "It's his. A graduation gift from my wife and me. A reward for his hard work. You know, he still has a hefty fine and the DUI. That's bad enough without the other charge."

"And you'll pay the fine, too," Skip said, flatly.

"Oh, no! No way. He's going to work it off. I own an asphalt paving business, so he'll be busy, believe me."

Skip nodded, watching the man's round animated face, which had the look of, *What do you say, Pal? Can we work something out here?*

"Sounds like just a summer job," Skip said, deflating the man's confidence. "Afraid I can't help you."

"Look," the man said, winding up for another pitch. "I know you have some physical issues. Why drag this out? It's just another headache for you."

"You didn't happen to lose a can of white paint did you?"

At that, Lucia who sat in the living room within earshot, smiled.

"What? No."

Confused for a moment, the man continued, "Can I at least get you to think about it? You'll be giving a deserving kid a second chance."

Skip held open the kitchen door.

As the man stepped outside, Skip said, "I thought about it when I pressed charges. Can't help you."

"Why you crazy old–"

Skip slammed the door.

The visitor knocked, causing Skip to yell, "Gloria, where's my shotgun?"

The man walked backward off the porch, swearing and calling Skip a, "spiteful old coot."

Gloria said, "Don't like salesmen, huh?"

Skip, with the shotgun in hand said, "I don't like what he's selling, that's for sure. Plus, I'm sure he got the kid a fancy lawyer, so he'll get off easy anyway."

Later, Skip and Gloria found Jamella with a broom in hand, standing in a cloud of golden barn dust.

Skip smiled.

"She does a great job. This is cleaner than my house."

"Not anymore," Gloria said, hands on hips.

Jamella pulled the scarf down covering her mouth and lifted the plastic safety goggles from her eyes.

"Who was that man? He seemed like a jerk."

"Salesman," Skip said, with a smirk.

"What did he want you to buy?"

"Horse manure,'" Skip said, nodding to a wheelbarrow filled with straw and horse poop. "Told him we had plenty."

Jamella's eyes brightened and the corner of her mouth curled into a slight smile.

"Ah!" Gloria said, pleased. "Nice to see you smile. You're usually so serious."

"I like to get my chores done."

"Best stable hand ever," Skip said, sitting on a hay bale.

"He drove just like the guy who ruined the sign," the girl said, slapping at the dust on her pants.

"Hmm," Skip nodded. "Like two peas in a pod. The law doesn't apply to them unless they're on the wrong end of it."

"He was mean-looking."

"That's a selfish person," Skip said. "They think they can get what they want by kissing fannies."

Jamella exchanged a confused look with Gloria, who clarified, "They take advantage of good people by pretending to be nice and polite."

"A sweet talker. You'd better be careful," Skip said, pointing to Jamella. "You're at the age where boys will sweet talk you, too. And you know for what..."

"We probably shouldn't talk about that," Lucia said, and Skip scoffed.

"I know about that already," Jamella said, as if it were no big deal.

Skip said to Lucia, "See? No flies on this kid."

Skip leaned his head back against the hay bale.

"Funny about the law. Sometimes it's broken by mistake or carelessness. Other times it's deliberate. That's wrong."

Lucia pressed her lips together.

Jamella stood next to the horse, her eyes wide.

"Come say 'Bye' to Cal," she said with her hand out, beckoning Lucia.

As she had with Skip, she wove her fingers within Lucia's and placed them by the horse's jaw. Cal's warmth and reassuring thump of its heart was soothing, and made time slow like the embrace of a loved one. Lucia rested her head against Cal's neck.

"I can see why you love this horse," she said, her eyes soft.

"Cal's a good one," Jamella said.

"You knew right along, huh, about me?"

"Was prison scary?"

Offhandedly, Lucia replied, "I don't recommend it."

To respect the sincerity of the girl's request, she added, "It was hard. I was sad for a very long time, and I missed out on many things."

"Like a family of your own?"

When she didn't reply, Jamella said, "But you have us, right?"

Skip sat on a hay bale, one hand holding a beer and the other on Ace's head. The dog rested against Skip's knee. The barn was quiet, cool, and a slight breeze was swirling bits of straw by the door. The old man's eyes were shiny dark, like the closed glass doors to a long, empty corridor.

"I do," Lucia said, her hand intertwined with Jamella's against Cal's neck. "Mister Skip has been very kind."

"He's been nice to me, too," Jamella said, "not like when I first came here."

"Oh?"

"Yeah, he talks with his heart now, instead of just his head."

"That's an amazing idea," Lucia said, patting Jamella on the shoulder. "He thinks with kindness."

"Uh·uh, like a family does."

"Having a family means a lot to you," Lucia said, moving away from Cal.

"I've never really had one until now," she said, spreading her arms to include all. "I like how real it feels. Before, I was just another kid in the house. I was an only. Now, I have a grandfather, Mister Skip, an aunt—you—and a mom and best friend, Hannah. All I need is a dad."

Lucia laughed.

"And I bet you have a plan for that. You're the needle pulling the thread."

"*Sí.* I like everything to be right," she said proudly.

Jesus arrived, the van's failing muffler rattling as he came to a stop near the house.

"Family is a wonderful goal," Lucia said, finishing her chat with Jamella. "My ride is here. Good night, Mister Skip."

Skip looked but didn't acknowledge her. His mind was with Eloise who he felt close to him.

Lucia was glad the pushy man had caught Skip when his mind was clear. Although, soon it would not make a difference since the old man was more forgetful and lost in his thoughts with each passing day. She worried about him at night, and had set up a daybed on the first floor, but he refused to use it, not even to nap. Lucia decided to ask Laura if she could stay with him overnight as well.

"Sure," Laura said, speaking with Gloria by phone later in the evening. "John told you to stay. I'll call him."

"Remind him that money's not a thing for me. Just want to do what's right."

John, seated in the shadows of his hotel room, answered Laura's call.

"Oh," she said, "I wasn't sure you'd pick up."

Wiping sweat from his forehead with a motel towel, he said, "Just got in."

Laura could tell by the echo of his voice the call was on the speaker setting of his cell phone.

"Is this a bad time?"

"No. Just back from a jog," he said, reaching to pull off a sneaker. "She's going to have to stay with him all the time, right?"

"She's going to sleep there, and said to not worry about what it will cost. She wants to help."

"I know."

He paused, took off the other sneaker, a blister forming on the big toe of his left foot.

"I'll be there tomorrow afternoon. She can have the rest of the weekend."

"Okay. I'll tell her," she said, about to end the call when John spoke up.

"Look, I just wished I'd have known."

He wanted to tell Laura how it was surreal having Lucia care for Skip, or how the feeling of being the lazy son who had let his dad down again had sparked his anger, but he said nothing. What difference would it make? Better to walk the straight line as Skip had suggested.

"I'm lucky to have you and well, her, too, as it turns out."

"Can't find anyone else?"

"No. Either no one wants to do it, or there's too much need. Weird system."

"It has been a struggle, I understand."

John sighed.

"I struggle with lots of things. Guess I'm a bit of a diva."

Laura chuckled, relieved by his attempt to laugh at himself.

"You're a work in progress," she said, "just like the rest of us."

"Thanks," John said, comforted by her words.

When he ended the call, the room's shadows lengthened, and an unusual quiet surrounded him. He would shower and pack a bag for the ride in the morning, accepting what he could not control or should have done better.

24

annah's mom, Kathy, was her daughter's twin. Both had shoulder length, thick blond hair, shiny, deep blue eyes, and pink cheeks.

"Hannah's different since she's been spending time here," she said with bright eyes. "She's more outgoing and happier since her grandfather died."

"For sure, the horse has something to do with it," Laura said.

"Right. Who doesn't love a horse? Thanks for letting her visit. She looks forward to it."

"Coffee?" Laura offered, thinking it was nice to have another parent in the kitchen.

They sat at the table and discussed the latest school news, places to shop, and events in town.

"Hard to buy clothes for Jamella now. She's fussy," Laura said, and they laughed. "Maybe we should take them shopping. It might be easier on both of us."

"If we can get them away from the barn long enough," Kathy said.

"Did I tell you I spoke to the vice principal about Jamella being bullied on the bus?"

"No," Kathy said, surprised. "Hannah never mentioned anything."

Laura, stirring milk into her cup said, "According to Jamella, Hannah's pretty good at dealing with it. Nice, too, to have an older brother."

"Oh, good. I'm glad he looks out for her. What did the VP say?"

Laura, holding the warm cup in her hands said, "That the parents were told if it continues, he's off the bus for the year and that the school resource officer would be alerted because Jamella's a minority student."

"Wow, that had to get their attention."

Laura nodded.

"I hope so."

"Who said parenting was easy? No one, ever."

Laura nodded.

They listened to the sounds of feet thumping against the ceiling.

After I bit, Laura said, "Looks like they'll be down in a minute."

"Thanks for the coffee," Kathy said, leaving an empty cup by the edge of the sink. "I'll be by later to get Hannah."

Kathy was no sooner gone when Laura heard the rumble of footsteps on stairs. She put two dirty cups in the sink and grabbed her jacket.

The girls ran out the back door, while Laura locked it and followed the road, happy that life with Jamella was finally a full circle. She smiled, waving to oncoming cars that lifted a cool breeze when they passed. She joined the girls, Lucia, and Skip as they led Cal from the barn and out onto the trail, which was wide enough for them to walk in pairs.

The horse led Jamella and Hannah down the path with the girls each holding the reins, a walk Cal knew well. It was overgrown in some places, but the horse deftly navigated around the thin, second growth maples, oaks, scrub pines, and shrubs. The path led downhill to a gravel opening along a shallow, wide brook flowing heavily with the normal spring swell. The cool air moved around them, following along with the tumbling, rolling water. Cal stopped, tipping his head to drink.

"This is a beautiful spot," Laura said, noting the yellow flowering, wild forsythia lining the opposite embankment.

A pair of small, red headed finches carried bits of straw and grass onto an overhanging pine tree limb where a brown nest sat. The path continued across the brook, but they would stop and talk while the girls explored a swirling pool ten feet downstream.

"When the water is lower, do you cross here?"

Skip nodded, aware of a growing buzzing sound moving closer.

"Damn," he said, looking to the opposite path.

"Sounds like dirt bikes," Laura said, as two riders stopped at the crest of the path, the flowing creek between them.

The riders wore black helmets, which hid their faces, jeans, long sleeved shirts and padding on their knees, elbows and wrists. One, the leader, was a male, his shoulders wide and his legs thick. The other was narrow-hipped and thin, a young woman.

"This is private property," Skip called, his voice shrill and strained. "Don't ride here. You're ruining the trails."

The male turned his bike sideways, and revved the throttle. Saluting them with the middle finger, he spun the rear tire, causing a cloud of dust and sand to rise into the air. A plume of sand, rock and gravel splashed heavily into the water, while the gray haze of exhaust floated across the stream. He drove off with the girl following behind.

"Damn trails are going to be rutted now and hard to walk," Skip said, with a punch of his fist.

"That was a girl," Jamella said, surprised. "Why is she acting like a jerk?"

"Guys, I get, but her, too?" Hannah added. "So rude!"

"They ran over the sign," Jamella said. "I saw them."

Skip turned to Lucia.

"See?" he said, and she nodded. "Glad I didn't give him a break. He'll get off easy enough with the uncle's fancy lawyer. Cash is king in this country."

The color in Skip's cheek faded. He sat on a tree stump, head down.

"Anyway, I need to put up new 'No Trespassing' signs."

"We'll help!" Jamella said, with Hannah nodding in approval.

"Why don't we head back," Lucia said. "It's almost noon."

Skip said to Lucia, "Your lawyer wasn't fancy, huh?"

Taken aback, Lucia replied, "No, but she tried hard. There was no reason to fight. I was a thousand percent guilty."

Skip nodded.

"I figured as much. Always appreciated how you owned up to it, unlike most."

John's car was parked near the house when they entered the clearing by the barn.

Lucia purposely walked the driveway to wait for Jesus' van by the side of the road.

Laura helped Skip to the porch where they met John.

"How are you holding up, Dad?"

"Arrgh," he said, with a wave of his hand.

"What's got into you?"

"Dirt bikers," Jamella said, "riding the trails."

"Ah, damn. We've got plenty of extra signs," John said. "Maybe after lunch, we put up a few. I'll show you the other trail access. It's a short ride from here."

John smiled, hoping Laura would agree, but she hesitated.

Laura sensed his attempt to smooth over the small fracture in their relationship and enjoyed letting him wait.

Finally, she agreed, and they planned a quick trip.

After driving a mile along a narrow and bumpy side country road, John parked in an opening by the trees and brush.

Jamella stepped out of the car, an empty, faded box of shotgun shells lay by her feet. Littered there were empty energy drink and beer cans along with plastic nip bottles, fast food wrappers, and cigarette butts.

"Gross," Jamella said, stepping gently between the littered mess.

"Hunters are usually good about their trash," John said, looking at the path into the woods, which was chewed up with knobbed tire ruts sunk into the wet earth.

The private property sign was missing.

"Not sure signage here would help, Dad. Maybe we need some type of barrier to go with it. Although, it's almost a quarter of a mile of access."

They walked the rutted path—Hannah and Jamella in front of John, Laura, and Skip—avoiding a deep, curved swale filled with ankle-deep rainwater made by ATV and dirt bikes at a bend in the woods. They came upon a small duck pond, built by beavers many years ago.

"My favorite spot," John said, as a brown mallard duck and six fluffy, down covered babies waddled into the water from the far side.

"Oh, Dad, I forgot to ask if you had a meeting with someone about the sign on the highway."

"A meeting with *who?*" Skip asked.

"I got a call last night from a lawyer. Said you met with his client about dropping the charges against the kid who ran over the sign. He said they were willing to offer a five-thousand dollar settlement."

The old man stared at his son, his jaw bobbing slightly as if he were to speak.

Finally, Jamella said with a tight smile, "The horse manure salesman," hoping to jog his memory.

"Bah, got plenty of that," Skip said, right hand twitching against the side of his leg.

"You were there?" Laura asked.

Jamella nodded.

"He was an older, jerky guy who came on Friday afternoon. Gloria was there, too. But Skip said he'd only get a fancy lawyer, and the one who ruined the sign wouldn't get in too much trouble."

Deliberately not naming Gloria, Laura added, "Good thing someone was with you, Skip."

John's eyes flashed.

"Some people have a lot of nerve. I'll be happy to tell that lawyer to go screw."

Jamella, with a slight smile, turned to Hannah and they giggled.

Skip sat on a rock, thinking of the beehives Eloise had kept under the maple trees on the far side where the water trickled into the brook. The hives were gone now. The old man could remember much from the past, but not why he was now here by the old hives.

A moment later and with a glint of amusement in his eyes he said, "Eloise raised bees. She would check on them when she went back and forth to work. Ha, got stung a few times, she did."

"They're nowhere to be found," John said, wringing his hands. "Someone obviously helped themselves."

Skip leaned forward as if to stand but said, "You know, Son, one bad moment shouldn't define a life."

John looked at Laura.

"Guess we're not talking about bees, huh?"

Skip pointed to Jamella and Hannah, who were now investigating the beaver dam near the pond's edge, and said, "Since she's come along, I've stopped looking back. Don't wait as long as I did, Son."

"Good advice," Laura said, cheerfully.

John took in the moment, then said, "I'm trying."

Skip opened his arms wide and with his palms up said, "Good. You have an opportunity here to make your mother and Libby happy."

"Not you, though?" Laura said to Skip, trying to lighten the mood.

"Me?" the old man said. "I'm fine, plus I'll be going soon."

"Where are *you* going?" John asked, sarcastically.

The old man cracked a smile, "McNally's Funeral Home."

His eyes brightened, proud of his joke.

They walked farther into the woods, where they found beer cans riddled with buckshot near a stump and a fire pit lined with old bricks.

"Not hunters after all," John said, kicking the bits of charred wood by the pit. "We're never going to stop kids from hanging out here."

"Sell," Skip said.

"What?"

"Along the road," Skip said, sweeping his right hand. "There's at least four acres you don't need."

"I'd rather try the signs."

"Nah," Skip said. "Almost 6 acres, shaped like a rectangle. Get a good price and be done with all that damn racket."

"It's not a bad idea," Laura said. "And there's always the chance someone *could* sue if there's an accident on your property."

John looked at the long stretch of woods along the road. Past the makeshift camp, the path narrowed. John rolled a few bowling ball-sized boulders and set some long, dead tree limbs across the width of the trail. He nailed a "Private Property" sign on a nearby tree trunk.

"At least the partiers are aware now," John said, hooking the hammer onto his belt.

They turned for home. The idea of selling the land as single-family lots made sense to John. He knew a surveyor and patted his dad's shoulder when they reached the road.

"You know, that's a great idea, Dad."

Skip, his eyes glazed over, didn't respond. He was lost in his thoughts.

John whispered to Laura, "He's in and out of it a lot."

Laura nodded, her eyes soft.

Behind them, Hannah and Jamella chatted happily, causing Laura to sense the bittersweet tug of wonder and sadness, death and life.

25

ucia was warming a leftover cheese pizza in the oven, when Andres knocked at the apartment door. He had arrived straight from a painting job he'd contracted. Andres slouched at the table, feet spread wide.

"Long day?" Lucia asked.

"Just finished. Owner let me start at six."

While they shared the pizza, Lucia noticed a streak of white paint in Andres' hair. She wet a rag and stood over him rubbing the patch that softened and released the smudge.

"Looks like there's a few gray ones in here," she teased.

He reached around and touched her bottom.

"I don't want to fall off the chair," he said. "You rub hard."

"And that's all I'm going to rub," she said, her voice firm.

"Playing hard to get?" Andres teased.

His cellphone rang. Fishing it out of a side coverall pocket, Lucia saw it was a woman calling. His wife.

"Go ahead," Lucia said. "I don't mind."

As Andres spoke, Lucia went out onto the back porch.

The college tenants were in the yard, sitting in a circle made of cheap lawn chairs, talking and laughing. Two of the men wore tee shirts with a landscaper's logo. They were sweaty. Their light green work shirts were covered with brown and green smudges. They spoke with the two women. One who wore the smock of a local big box store, while the other had on the black and white outfit of a restaurant server. They were exchanging stories of their workday, each listening to the others' stories. The spring semester had ended, and they would spend the summer working, complaining, talking, and laughing.

Lucia wished she had taken her schooling seriously. Instead, she developed the habit of humor and silliness, to avoid feeling or looking stupid in front of her peers. She struggled with learning English when she was young and fell behind with reading. Rather than digging in, she chose to deflect attention by making a joke or pretending not to understand. She did enough schoolwork to keep her parents happy, but sold herself short. *I gave up on myself.*

When Andres stepped onto the porch, he wore a frown. "The little man is giving my wife a hard time."

"Echa de menos a su papá," Lucia said. "How long since he's been with you?"

"Mucho tiempo," Andres said, leaning against the wall. "I miss him, too. We talk over the computer, but it's not the same."

"So, what will you do? Can you bring them here?"

"No," Andres sighed, "but maybe Canada. They are better. 'Express Entry' it's called. Going to give it a try."

Lucia wrapped her arms around her chest and shivered. With a smile she said, "Ah, but it's so cold there!"

Andres laughed.

"It is, but it's safe to live, no? You were lucky to be born here."

"I know," she said. "I took it for granted. I was too bothered by what others thought of me. Silly."

Lucia took his hand.

"Canada's a good idea."

"Yes," he said.

Andres squeezed Lucia's palm with both hands.

"And what will you do?"

"You mean without my *amigo hermoso?*" she teased.

"There's an empty chair down there," she said, pointing to the yard below. "I will join them. Maybe be a nurse."

"I'll still be around for you," he said, releasing her hand. "For a while, at least."

But Lucia knew she would eventually stop replying immediately to his texts, and they would drift apart. Although she would miss Andres, it would give her more time to spend with Jesus, Maria, Roberto and focus on a new career. Once she moved past the upcoming week, which would be intense with having to care for Skip night and day, she would have time to work on herself. Like the students below, Lucia's future finally had a direction.

She would need her driver's license reinstated, though, which she was still reluctant to do. The idea of sitting behind the wheel of a car brought the intrusive thoughts of waking in the hospital after the crash. It also reminded her of the crushing humiliation of standing before a judge with her shocked and teary-eyed family present, which could easily be triggered again. It would have to be done gradually.

Lucia arrived at Skip's on Monday morning with an overnight bag and a bit of anxiety, prompted by John's car in the driveway.

"Good luck, Little Sister," Jesus said, as she stepped from the van. "Do you want me to go inside?"

Lucia shook her head.

"I'll call you tonight."

When she entered the kitchen, Skip was seated at the table with a cup of coffee and two pieces of plain-buttered toast.

"See? I told you she'd be back," John said.

Skip raised a hand to greet her, then slid the toast to her.

"Good morning," Gloria said. "Need a little something on those, huh?"

Taking a plate of avocado slices from the refrigerator, she placed three pieces on each piece of bread.

Skip said, "Finally, some decent food."

While Skip ate, John and Gloria stepped into the living room.

John said, "I get what you're trying to do. I appreciate it, but I can't forget what happened. It'll always be that way, but I realize we're different now, and Dad likes having you. It's the damnedest thing, isn't it?"

Lucia was unsure how to respond.

John added, "I mean, life, fate, *too* strange to understand."

She nodded, refusing to let the words, "I'm sorry," slide between her lips. She had apologized enough. It was time to make amends, instead.

"There's a room to the left at the top of the stairs," John said, motioning to her overnight bag.

"How was his weekend?" Gloria asked.

"He keeps going on about how this is his last week," John said, bemused. "He thinks it's funny, I guess. He is failing though, weaker, and can't keep his thoughts together. But he asked about you. Likes you more than me, for sure."

"We get along," Lucia said. "He's a gentle man. A good man."

Her eyes filled with emotion, so she turned her face away.

"I know. I used to think his 'One foot in front of the other' idea was nonsense, but it's about the only way."

Lucia, wiping her eyes with a tissue said, "It is, and having something to look forward to helps."

"Will you stay on after this week?"

"Yes."

Later, as John drove to the office, he returned the lawyer's call, letting him know that under no circumstances would his father drop the charges for the damage done to the sign.

"Are you sure?" the man said. "I'm told your dad has health issues. Is he really thinking..."

"It doesn't matter to him. He's pretty black and white when it comes to the law."

"That's disappointing," he said, but quickly added, "in this case, I mean."

"Please let your client know that we don't want any more unannounced visits, either. It upsets my dad."

Hannah spent Friday night and Saturday morning with Jamella and Laura. Hannah loved the horse, the barn, Ace, and the freedom of being on her own.

On Monday, Jamella explained to Lucia how they had become friends as she brushed Cal in the barn.

"She let me sit next to her on the bus," the girl said. "She didn't stare or ask weird questions. She just read her book."

"A good friend for you. She has courage."

"Why don't some people like our color?"

Lucia sighed.

"No good reason. Pretty stupid, isn't it?"

"They're scared."

Jamella handed the grooming brush to Gloria.

"You try it."

Gloria mimicked how Jamella had used the brush.

"What were your friends like?"

"All silly," Lucia said. "We weren't good students like you and Hannah. We cared more about clothes and boys than books."

"We have those types, too. I'm not into that but it would be nice to know how to fix this hair—too frizzy. If it's cut short, I look like a boy, and when it's long I have a brown mushroom growing on top of my head."

Lucia laughed.

She stopped brushing Cal, her arm holding the brush fell to the side.

"Have you had your hair done?"

"Mom wants me to go to her stylist, but I don't want to. Where do you go?"

"Are you serious?"

She handed the wooden brush to Jamella.

"My hair's a mess, but I could ask my niece, Maria. She'd know where young people go."

"Who look like we do, right?"

"Yes," Lucia said, watching a pleased Jamella's eyes curl upward as part of a tight smile.

Lucia had not had her hair done since the short haircut she had asked for in prison. She understood Jamella wanting her hair to look authentic, even if she would be the only girl in the school or community with a unique style.

"We can talk to mom about it."

26

The news of Skip rejecting a settlement caused a stir. Gloria woke to see the old man sitting in an oak wood chair by his back bedroom window holding a gun. The buzzing of dirt bikes deep in the woods after midnight addled him. His shuffling out of bed to sit by the window with the shotgun had roused Lucia.

Skip's eyes shone in the soft moonlight that lit the corral and barn like sheer cloth over a lampshade.

"Mister Skip," Lucia said softly, standing by his open bedroom door. "Everything okay?"

Skip grunted. The reality of a man with worsening dementia holding a loaded firearm was unsettling.

"Coming closer," he said, although the engines buzzing had softened.

"Slow now," he added, lifting the window screen.

Two flashlight beams shone upon the weathered barn's wood planks, but the light was too far to reach the house. The riders dismounted, bikes idling, and crept slowly forward. Skip aimed the gun up into the night and fired. The bang caused Lucia to jump.

The flashlights went off.

Within seconds, the bikes revved, and they drove off by the wooded trails.

Skip slid the screen down.

"Sorry to wake you," he said with a smirk.

"That was loud!"

"Never fired a gun, have you?"

"No," Lucia said, noting the clarity in Skip's eyes.

"Does come in handy, though, when you're my age," he said, setting the safety lock.

He gave her the weapon.

"Here, a crazy old man shouldn't have a gun."

"No. But you weren't going to shoot them," Lucia said with a nervous chuckle.

"Only if I had to," he said matter-of-factly.

Laying back onto the bed he said, "Keep that in your room. If they come back, do what I just did," and he closed his eyes.

Lucia's hands trembled as she leaned the gun against the back wall in her room's closet. The bang of the shot tingled through her. No chance she would ever use the rifle. Sitting on the bed, she listened for the dirt bikes, but heard nothing. Before falling off to sleep, she marveled at how Skip could be so sharp-minded despite spending most of the day in a mental fog. Adrenaline maybe? She would call Jesus in the morning and ask him to add a security camera to the back of Skip's house, while he was installing one for Laura. Skip was not fazed by the intrusion, but Lucia was alarmed by the riders' brazenness.

The next day, when talking with Jesus about the arrogance and sense of entitlement of the bikers, her brother scoffed.

"Nothing's changed, Little Sis. It's America. White people," he said with a shake of his head. "We know how that goes."

"But why trouble a little girl and an old man?" Lucia said, waiting as her brother downloaded the "app" for the wireless cameras on Skip's home to Lucia's phone.

"Water seeks its own level," he said before showing Lucia how the cameras were controlled from her phone. "They're just cowards."

"Reminds me of prison," she said, thinking of the overt and subtle bullying she had experienced.

"Maybe we're all in jail. We just don't know it," Jesus snickered. "Free but not free. Anyway, with this," he said, "you can get good pictures even at night. Better than a gun because you can show the police. See?"

Lucia's phone held multiple pictures of Lucia and Jesus standing near the house after the cameras were activated.

"You might want to hide the bullets," he said, "just in case. He was in Vietnam, right?"

Lucia nodded.

"I'll keep an eye on it."

With a sly look he asked, "How's Andy?"

"A little preoccupied with *su hijo* not behaving, but I don't plan on seeing him much. It's not the right thing for his family."

"And," Jesus said, as he placed two screwdrivers in his back pocket, "you've got your hands full here...for now."

"Yes, but it's only tough when he talks to himself. He gets very agitated sometimes. It worries me."

"All the more reason to hide the ammo, huh?" he said, patting her shoulder.

He then turned and went to his truck.

"Next week, driving school," he said with a smile, pointing to the van. "The new instructor is *loco,* but you might like him."

Skip sat on the rocker, watching Cal eating grass out in the field.

He asked, "Who was that?"

"My brother," she said, deciding not to remind Skip he had met Jesus two hours ago. "We can see who's on the property now. Won't have to shoot anybody," she teased. "We'll show the police instead."

"I did enough shooting a long time ago," he said, while nodding in agreement. "Don't recommend it."

"Not something I'd want to do, either."

Skip pointed a thin finger.

"They're in the field there."

"Who?" Lucia asked, suddenly alarmed. "Those who came last night?"

The old man's hollow eyes remained fixed.

"My men. The ones who didn't come home. They're smiling now."

Lucia followed the aim of his index finger.

"Oh? Hmm. That's nice I guess—like good news, bad news, huh?"

"I wish I would've known they'd be okay after I came home," he said, wiping at the corner of his left eye. "Would've slept a lot better."

They sat on the porch, Skip in a rocker, Lucia on the top step, his eyes glazed and fixed beyond the barn and field to a world only he could see.

On a whim, she asked, "What's in my future?"

Without hesitation, he said flatly, "Wonder and sadness, like everybody else. Until the end. Then you'll see how it all comes together."

"Do you know this because of your faith?"

"No," Skip said with an emphatic shake of his head. "It's like this. How many stars can you see during the day? One, right...the sun. At night, you see them all. That's what it's like when this life and the next are close together. Religion is about only one star, that's nothing. At the end, our soul lets us see what the brain can't."

Lucia stood.

"That's interesting."

"It sure is," he said, as she helped him to his feet. "Wish I'd known when I was younger. Now all of this," he said, making a small circle in the air with a shaky right hand, "is just a step along the way."

Teasingly, she said, "So we're better off dead."

"Sure seems that way," he said, pausing for one more look at the field.

As if speaking to ghosts in his mind he added, "When I die, I'll live on in the stories others tell until they're gone, too."

A fresh gust of air, heavy with the scent of the purple lilacs growing by the side of the porch, made Skip pause. Ace sniffed the air, yawned, then rose from the shady spot by the rocker. As they walked to the corral fence, Ace shuffled alongside. At the fence, Skip fed a carrot to Cal, while Ace looked on in anticipation. Skip was content, at ease, feeling his release from the physical world was at hand.

While Lucia was sure his thoughts were based on a loosely toggled brain, his comfort gave her pause. What if death was nothing to fear? Living could be painful, unfair, and a heavy burden. However, even a soft landing in the afterlife would not justify one's suffering in this world.

Ace, seated at Skip's feet, barked. The old man shakily pulled a treat from his pocket.

Standing with her hands dangling over the top rail, Lucia asked, "So what's the key to this world?"

Skip turned to Lucia and lightly grabbed her wrist.

With a finger against the burn scar Lucia had made years ago when in despair, he said, "Kindness. We are our brothers' keepers above all. It's a shame that what *doesn't* matter distracts us from it."

John was in the habit of speaking by phone to Laura every night. At first, to check on Skip, but their conversations lasted for an hour or more. He was unaware of the midnight visitors Skip had chased away, a fact Laura kept from him so he could focus on work. John told

Laura he missed her, and of Lucia he said, "I guess this was fate's way of telling me to move on, to live life. I wasn't much use to anyone—including myself—for a long time."

He spoke with Jamella, asked about Cal, Hannah, and Ace. He thanked her for cleaning the barn and offered to take her for lunch on Saturday, but Jamella declined. She had a date with mom, Gloria and Hannah to get their hair styled.

"Sounds like fun," he said, reacting to the excited timber of her voice.

"You're dad's doing okay, too," she said, "in case you were wondering."

John, amused by her sarcasm said, "Oh really? Guess you're keeping him in line."

"Do you really like my mom?"

"What? Sure..."

"Because you're taking a long time."

John heard Laura say in the background, "Don't bother him about that."

He chuckled.

"Your mom will be a priority as soon as I'm done here. Do you need any feed or supplies for the barn?"

"No," she said, handing the phone to Laura.

John said, "She's all business, huh? I better get a move on then."

"We can figure that out when you're back in a few days."

27

The remainder of the week was quiet, much to Lucia's relief. She was glad to leave the rifle hidden in the closet. Keeping herself busy with laundry, cooking, and cleaning helped her feel productive and busy. She was up with the sun to visit with Jamella in the barn, whose early routine included providing fresh water, a bit of feed, and a good morning hello before walking with Cal to the field.

When finished, Jamella kicked off her vinyl "barn boots" as she called them, before heading to hop onto the school bus.

The mornings were tranquil for Lucia, who sat with Skip on the back porch as they sipped coffee.

Skip sometimes acting normally, other times gesturing and talking to imaginary visitors, none of it related to his prior career, but with those he had known during Vietnam.

Lucia was content to watch Cal as he swished his tail and nibbled the grass. The horse's lean, muscled neck flashed in the sunlight, his profile highlighted by the green-leaved, wooded backdrop of gray bark, wild shrubs, and tall pines. For Lucia, the space in front of her was as wide as eternity, and if not for the old man's chatter, just as soundless. She thought of the days alone in her cell and how she could never have imagined such calm or felt such peace.

Filling her lungs with cool morning air, she sighed, her thoughts of prison drifting away. Her day would begin after their first cup of coffee, when she would make breakfast. Later, she would go about the routine of keeping Skip's home, all the while keeping an eye on the old man, who wasn't prone to wander, but didn't watch television.

His thoughts were his own and he needed a plain tapestry upon which to project them. Sitting on the porch or by the front bay window, Skip rummaged through the baggage of his mind, while affording Lucia the time to do what was needed.

She worried more, lately, as his appetite decreased, so she served chocolate protein shakes for him to sip in the afternoon.

On Thursday evening, Lucia, Skip and Jamella were in the barn with the old man seated on the worn-round hay bale spot that he liked, when Jamella asked if Lucia would take a picture. She brought Cal over to Skip, leaned against his side, put her hand on Skip's shoulder and smiled as Lucia sighted the cellphone. Jamella insisted on a nearly impossible "selfie" which did manage to include them, but at weird angles, which made them laugh. After repeated tries, Jamella finally settled on one picture.

"Send it to my email," Jamella asked. "I'm going to make it bigger like a family portrait."

Jamella patted Ace on the head and said, "This is the best, *ever*. I've made so many friends."

"And you have a nice home," Lucia said, as Skip nodded in agreement. "Almost two homes, huh? Pretty lucky."

Jamella smiled.

"Yes, and I have a good friend now, too. Hannah."

"It's Cal's birthday," Skip said, his eyes now refocused on Lucia and Jamella.

He responded to Jamella's question of how old the horse was by saying, "I don't know, but we got him in April."

"It's May second," Lucia said, "Cal's overdue for a party."

"He likes cucumbers, carrots, and apples," Skip said. "We can feed him some from Eloise's garden."

Jamella asked, "What garden?"

"Sure, we can," Lucia said, smiling at Jamella. "Maybe on Saturday morning before we leave for our girls' afternoon. It's all set with my niece. We're going to a salon she recommended."

Jamella's eyes were blank as thoughts rolled around in her mind, not the response Lucia expected.

"Aren't you excited?"

Jamella shrugged.

"I'm not sure what to ask for. Like what style I want."

"Don't worry. My niece Maria will help us."

A low snore came from Skip, whose head rested against the barn wall.

Jamella picked up a one-gallon galvanized pail by the old man's feet.

"I got an idea," she said, looking into the empty bucket. "We can have a party!"

Excitement built as the week went on for Jamella. She wrapped the pail in light blue craft paper and then placed apples, cucumbers, celery, strawberries, and carrots in it.

On Saturday morning, she and Hannah carried the bucket and two blue and white streamers along with a "Happy Birthday, Cal" poster to the barn.

While the horse lolled in the field, the girls readied a surprise. Streamers hung above his corral and the hand drawn poster of Cal was placed on the barn wall. The pail filled with goodies for Cal was hidden behind the hay.

Laura laughed when Jamella clapped the dirt from her hands, the girl's head nodding with approval over the decorated stall.

Turning to Hannah she said, "This is like the best day ever so far!"

The girls scampered from the barn to find Cal, Skip, and Gloria.

Laura paused for a moment, the feelings of a happy daughter warmed her heart, as did, finally, a woman feeling like a mom. She had taken Jamella to shop for streamers, paper goods, and produce for the pail, the whole time debating, deciding, and discussing how to best prepare for Cal's birthday.

"I never thought hanging out with a horse could be so much fun!" Jamella said, as the two carefully placed layers of celery, carrots, cucumbers, apples and strawberries in the pail.

Laura would not have guessed so much could change by following an uneven, uphill path from her backyard to a scary old barn whose grumpy owner would help Jamella climb out of her shell. Although the tween was still easily distracted and hated loud noises, Jamella had learned to get her schoolwork done, ask a question when she needed to, and make a best friend in Hannah. Laura's life felt full, authentic, and the worry of adopting a foster, biracial child was eased now thanks to Skip, Cal, and Gloria—all strangers four months ago. She wondered if it was just a coincidence of fate, as John believed, or was it what Jamella had subconsciously desired and found?

Laura walked through the barn door and into the sunlight. John's car was in the yard, and her heart jumped. The girls led Cal to the opening in the corral, while Lucia walked with Skip toward the barn.

John carried a suitcase to the house. Lucia had placed a travel bag with straining zippers onto the porch.

"Two ships passing," he said softly.

He left a suitcase and a soft jean duffle bag stuffed with dirty laundry on the porch near Lucia's. Stepping back, he noted the irony. He had given up with health care agencies because Skip had insisted on keeping Gloria and maybe, "to help the woman out."

"Help *her* out? What the hell's gotten into you? When did you become Mister Nice Guy?"

Skip paused.

"When Miss J came along,'" he said, with conviction. "Got me thinking about what I've done and what I should have been doing."

"So now you're going to save the world?"

Skip waved a hand dismissively.

"Bah. Not interested in your drama. It's not like I'm asking for the moon."

John was surprised to see how slowly Skip walked—head bent forward, small, slow, tentative steps across the yard—in only a week's time. John turned from the porch as the faraway buzz of dirt bikes riding the trails exasperated him. He wondered how many of the private property signs had been flamed in a campfire.

Skip walked with Lucia to the barn like lifelong friends. Skip gestured with a shaky hand as he spoke and Lucia politely nodded. She patiently pointed to uneven spots while gently supporting his weight.

For the casual observer, Skip and Lucia were an old man and a kind aide, without prior history. Like a shiny, plate glass window, the optics of the present overcame those from the past.

Skip had forgiven Gloria and thank God, or John would have had to give up his promotion.

Lucia had redeemed herself in the best way possible. She made Skip happy in his final days.

John would plan a new day schedule with her so she could stay on working days. He caught up with Skip and Lucia as they entered the barn. John frowned when he heard Skip talking aloud then intently listening to only what the old man could hear.

"How long has this been going on?" John asked.

"It's gotten worse this week. He has full conversations now," Gloria said.

She sat Skip on his well-worn bale of hay. Everyone wore small, pointy party hats including Ace and Cal, whose hat was tied with string under its jaw. The horse sniffed when the pail was placed at its feet.

"Happy birthday, Cal!" Jamella said, as Hannah offered pieces of a red apple to the horse. Jamella hugged the horse's neck, and stroked Cal's cheeks as it chewed. They sang the "Happy Birthday" song with some enthusiasm, the girls' voices loud and strong.

John stood by Laura and with an arm around her shoulders, he pulled her to his side.

"Nice to see you," he said.

She rested her head on his chest.

"I want you and Jamella to come with me tomorrow. I want to take dad out to lunch. Give him a break. If he's up to it. If not, how about a coffee run and some doughnuts. What do you say?"

Laura laughed.

"Gee, sounds fancy. We'll be ready."

Before the party broke up, John sat with Lucia.

"Can you stay on days now? Monday to Friday? And we have to settle what I owe you for your time. This is a surreal conversation, huh? I mean, did you ever think we'd be, uh..."

"No. Never expected this," she said, using a tissue to wipe a bit of spit from the side of Skip's face.

"Right. Who would have? How's that prayer go, about granting us the serenity to accept what can't be changed? Looks like it's become our lot in life."

"I'm fortunate. Your father has been good to me."

"How so?" John said, removing his party hat.

"His forgiveness gives me hope."

John ignored the frustration rising within him. Again, his father, a man who seemed always to do the right thing, outdid him. Lifelong, he had sought the approval of a man who was not easy. Skip was not especially difficult, but his sarcasm sometimes left a mark. It was Eloise who had comforted her son, noticed his good work, and who stepped in when he struggled. Once she passed, the old man and his son were left to rub together like porcupines in a suitcase.

Moving in front of Skip, he remembered the five pack of double stuffed Oreos he had bought at the convenience store crowded into his front pants pocket. He tore the wrapper and handed one each to Skip and Lucia.

"Going to need milk with these," he said, beating his dad to the remark, but Skip didn't respond.

Instead, he stared at the cookie sitting on his palm, as did Lucia.

Skip raised his eyes, taking a long look at his son's face.

"Go ahead, Dad. Those are your favorites."

Skip snapped off a bite and chewed.

"Stale," he said and they laughed.

John gave the other two to Jamella and Hannah, who swallowed them in one bite.

"Come on," Lucia said, patting Skip on the shoulder. "Let's go. Time for meds. Maybe have a glass of milk, too."

She slowly led him to the barn door.

After swallowing her cookie, Hannah said to Jamella, "Are you going to ask him?"

"Ask me what?" John said.

Jamella nodded.

After taking a deep breath, she began, "There's a dance at school for parents. I can ask mom, but most girls bring their dads. Would you bring me?"

"You want me? Sure, that's quite an honor, if it's okay with your mom."

"Oh!" Jamella said. "Mom told me I could ask."

"We'll go with my dad," Hannah said while smiling, palms pressed together.

"Why do I think this was planned a while ago?" John teased.

"Because it was," Laura said, moving to pick up the party hats. "Girls, can you take Cal's bucket into Mister Skip's kitchen? Time to get ready to go."

"Big plans?" John asked as the girls skipped from the barn, each holding the handle of the pail with one hand.

"Yup. Their first hair styling appointment. Girls only, sorry."

John chuckled.

"That's fine."

Handing his party hat to Laura, he said, "We need to make some time together, too."

"We do," she said.

They paused, neither knowing what to say, when the buzzing of dirt bikes grew louder.

"I'll take Cal to the field. I want to see what's going on with those damn bikes."

Lucia and Skip had cleared the path between the barn and the house when Skip looked back, then stopped.

"We should get inside," Lucia said, hoping to keep the old man calm.

Skip patted her hand.

"Don't worry. You'll be okay," he said.

John, Cal, and Ace were by the corral gate, when the grating buzz from the bikes' engines made them stop.

Hannah and Jamella heard a commotion and looked through the kitchen window. The bikes' exhaust created a bluish haze that moved snakelike along the path. They watched as two riders came from the woods, their engines screaming.

Cal reared up as they approached, causing the first driver to swerve to the side. Its back tire fired a plume of gravel and stone at Skip and Lucia. The trailing biker, unable to control the front wheel, tumbled to the ground at John's feet.

"John!"

28

He turned to see Laura kneeling next to Skip and Lucia, who lay together, Skip atop Lucia. The two girls stood behind her, hands to their faces.

"John!" Laura called again.

Lucia lay stunned.

Skip was dead.

Stepping in front of Lucia as the riders approached, a bullet-shaped stone had penetrated the base of his skull. He died instantly, the force of the blow knocking them to the ground.

"Dad!" John said. "What the hell?"

The ooze of blood on Skip's collar confused him.

Lucia picked a grain of sand from her right eye.

"Mister Skip!" she said, wiggling out from under the man. "Oh, no!"

The fallen rider stood, lifting the bike, which had stalled. Walking alongside it, the biker goosed the throttle.

John, unsure of what had happened, knew enough not to let the rider leave. Covering the distance in three long strides, he grabbed for the leather collar and pulled. Surprisingly, there was little resistance.

He jumped upon the rider's chest, and realized the biker was a girl. He tore off the helmet of a young white woman, possibly nineteen years of age. Her black pupils were wide with adrenaline.

In anger, John raised the helmet and said, "What's wrong with you! Why would you do this?" and punctuated each question by slamming the helmet against the front tire's rim.

"John!" Laura said, "Please come here."

Jamella stood with a cellphone near Hannah, who had tears in her eyes.

"The police and rescue are coming. Mom, they want to talk to you."

"Don't go anywhere," John said to the rider.

"I can't! You ruined it," the girl said of the tire.

John pinned her to the ground with a hand to her throat. "Stay down!"

As if struck by lightning, Hannah flung herself at the rider—"Arrgh!"—Hannah's fists pummeling the rider's head and shoulders.

John pulled the hysterical girl away but not before Hannah screamed at the rider, "I *hate* you!"

Lucia's nose bled. Her face was scraped and scratched. She sat with the old man's head in her lap. Stunned, she stroked Skip's cheek as if he were comfortably sleeping.

John knelt by his dad, feeling for the base of his skull. The rock had made a clean, deep two-inch hole. The old man's eyes were gray, blank, and his pulse was flat.

"Aww, no, no . . ." He grabbed Skip's hand and squeezed.

He placed his forehead against the old man's and moaned.

Moving Skip into John's arms allowed Lucia to crawl away, roll to her knees, and then stand. Lucia frantically wiped the blood from her hands onto her pant legs. She felt only a cool, dry trickle of blood from the right nostril.

Noticing the rock embedded in Skip's skull, she remembered the thump of the strike and the force of Skip's body upon hers. Lucia, arms wrapped around her waist and her eyes darting wildly from Skip to the biker, the girls, and then to Laura felt the fury of confusion within her.

Lucia howled, "God! No! Why?"

She fell to her knees sobbing and muttering, "No, no, please, no."

A darkness she had not felt since her first nights in prison made her body shake uncontrollably.

"Oh, Mister Skip, why? Why did you save *my* life?"

Cal stuck a skittish nose into Skip's shoulder, nudging the old man forward then back against his son's chest. John wanted to shoo the horse away but stopped when he saw its damp eyes. Cal nudged Skip twice, but the old man didn't respond, nor did he move when Ace placed his head on Skip's legs, eyes hopeful.

"He's gone," John said quietly to Laura, who knelt by his side.

As Laura's breathing calmed, she caressed Skip's forehead, the result of the accident settling around her like broken glass. Regaining her composure, she imagined the thoughts and feelings swirling within John. The tragic unfairness his family had suffered. The grief endured from the unexpected losses of love and life, and the constant feeling of being hounded by a horrible and unsympathetic shroud of doom. Worse, he never had the chance to say good-bye properly to his daughter, mother, or father. She looked to see Jamella directing emergency vehicles as they arrived to where Skip lay, and tears came to Laura's eyes. She stayed with John, who cradled his dad, and cried without shame.

The first to arrive was Sergeant Wilson.

After meeting briefly with John he said, "This is a crime scene. We'll need statements from all of you."

He handcuffed the female rider and placed her in the cruiser for "Trespassing," Wilson said.

More medical personnel came, but it was the female state medical examiner who arrived later to pronounce Skip dead.

The old man was left to lay where he had fallen, a white sheet covering his body, while police detectives stepped around him taking notes and recreating the scene.

Jamella, no longer focused on the logistics of directing emergency responders, said of Skip's body, "You can't leave him like that, hey! Please don't cover his face!"

When no one responded, she walked under the caution tape surrounding him and knelt at his side. She pulled the sheet from his head and shoulders. She kissed his forehead, tears from her eyes falling upon his cheeks. Jamella then curled up next to him and rested her head upon his heart.

Hannah followed Jamella and sat with her legs crossed, a hand gently placed upon the thin hair of Skip's head.

Wilson then directed the forensics team to work around the body.

"Thank you," Hannah's mom, Kathy, said to Wilson.

She was red faced from rushing on foot up the driveway.

"They need a little more time," he said to Kathy of the detectives on the scene.

Jamella insisted—and Wilson allowed it—that Skip's face not be covered, even after he was placed on a gurney and into the ambulance.

Hannah, Jamella, and their moms, each took a turn squeezing Skip's leg to say goodbye.

"He doesn't look dead," Jamella said, the fatal wound hidden as he lay on his back. "I wish he could stay."

"I do, too," Laura said, her physical energy sapped.

"Oh!" Jamella said, remembering her promise to care for the horse. "We have to check on Cal."

John sat with his dad in the ambulance after speaking to the medical examiner.

"It happened so fast. There was no pain," the ME had said, which was some comfort.

Of the many thoughts swirling in his head, John settled on one. Dad hadn't suffered, and his end was dignified.

"You saved her," he said, placing his hand on Skip's forehead.

He smiled as a tear came to his eye. *You forgave.*

"He was a good guy," Wilson said, standing by the van doors.

"Thanks," John said.

And he was a better man, too.

John stood by as the ambulance's engine revved. As he watched the van roll away, his eyes turned to the house, old and in need of upkeep. What had been—teaching Libby to ride a horse, pulling weeds for Eloise, helping clean the barn, or learning from Skip how to drive "a stick", was replaced by the spent, faded, and tired. The happy, joyful memories of his time as a boy stood before him like the tilted, timeworn headstones of the dead.

"We're going to arrest the other rider," Wilson said. "The video from the cameras should nail him."

"It's the same kid who ruined the sign," John said, repeating what he had heard from Jamella.

Wilson nodded.

"We're taking the aide—Gloria, right?—to be evaluated. She's in rough shape up here," he said, pointing to his temple. "Physically, she's fine."

Lucia was inconsolable, especially after Jesus arrived.

She repeated, "Why would he save my life?" whenever asked for her version of the accident, as if that was all that mattered.

Jesus insisted she take the transport to the hospital.

"Let them check you out," he said. "I'll be right there."

She agreed.

His last words to her were, "Try to relax."

Lucia was given a mild tranquilizer through an IV drip. She closed her eyes and concentrated on the technician's advice to breathe deeply. Lucia had no idea what it was like to be struck by lightning, but the electric shaking of her arms and legs along with the thumping of her heart, was as close as one got and survived. She spent the evening at the hospital with her brother, and Maria and Roberto.

Before leaving, Jesus patted Lucia's shoulder.

He said, "He wanted you to *live*. In time, you'll know why."

After they left, she turned onto her side and fell into a deep, dreamless, medicated sleep.

John, Laura and Jamella had a dinner of leftover meatloaf and corn salad from Skip's fridge. They ate quietly, each absorbed in their thoughts of the day.

The spell was finally broken when they all went to the barn and John said, "Dad laid a suit out on the bed with the paperwork from the funeral home."

"He told us he was leaving soon," Jamella said matter-of-factly as she placed grain in Cal's feedbag. "He told us not to worry."

"He did mention that," John said. "Always prepared. A seventy-nine-year-old boy scout."

"He wasn't much for first impressions," Laura said without bitterness. "A bit grumpy."

"He was mad the day I picked up his trash!" Jamella said, but a fast-moving cloud of sadness settled over her. "If I hadn't made the sign none of this would've happened."

Leaning over, she hugged the dog, arms around its neck.

Laura gently corrected her.

"*We* made the sign," she said, making a twirling motion with her index finger.

"No one expected something like this," John said. "You made my dad happy, Jamella. Remember that."

"He was like my own grandfather...," Jamella's lips shuddered. "And Gloria, too, I'll never see her. Nothing ever lasts!" she said, kicking the dirt.

John looked at Laura.

"Maybe this time it will."

"You're just saying that."

He put a hand on her shoulder and said, "It's time for things to be settled. One day at a time. Ha, now I sound like my dad."

"He surprised me,'" Laura said. "I didn't think he could change."

At that, they returned to the house and cleared off the kitchen table, plates and silverware clinking together, and then went into the living room.

Once seated in his father's recliner, John rubbed his hands upon the armrests, as if taking from it the essence of the man who had sat upon its cushions for many years.

John said, as if alone, "When he was rude to you two, I almost didn't recognize him. He would never have spoken like that before." He paused to rub his eyes. "But then Jamella set him straight, right?"

With a sideways smirk the girl said, "We argued a little at first."

"I'm glad you did," John said. "The way he spoke to you was not like him. Living alone drew the life out of him."

"And he was sad," Jamella said, "like you."

John nodded.

"I was a lot of things for a long time. I expected life to be fair, but that was dumb. It's not, but you know that better than me, huh?" he said to Jamella, whose eyes flashed like someone who knew much more than a girl her age should.

They sat quietly now at the end of a day that had begun with so much promise. Jamella's left hand traced silhouettes on the couch cushion.

John asked, "You'll still take care of Cal, right?"

"But Ace will be lonely," the girl said.

"Maybe I can take him to the office. Sleeps a lot, right?"

The girl dropped her head.

"It was so perfect!" she said with frustration.

"You're right to be upset," John said. "We all are."

"Hate chases me," she said plainly. "I'm sorry, Mom," the girl added, noting her mother's reaction, "but it's true. I'm different and if it wasn't for Hannah, I'd have no friends at all."

Jamella would have difficulty drawing for the remainder of the spring, her mind clouded by darkness and loss. Even Cal and Ace, when drawn, had long, distended legs as if both had bled out.

Laura offered no reply to Jamella's comment. Instead, the guilt she felt for bringing a brown-black child into her white world had suddenly dug so deeply into her gut that she struggled to think.

John said, "Hannah and my dad *chose* you, Jamella. They don't give friendship away. It means you earned it. These other kids will never know what it means to have such a good friend."

Regaining some composure, Laura suggested that John sleep on the couch at her house.

"Might be best if we spent tonight under one roof," she said. "I've got plenty of sheets and pillows."

Later, at midnight, Jamella rose and crawled into Laura's bed.

29

Earlier in the evening, John confirmed with the funeral director that only a small church mass was what Skip had wanted.

"No wake. I can't do that again," he said to Laura while seated in her kitchen. "Everyone was kind, but it sucked the life out of me. I needed to grieve, but had to stand for hours. I had no energy for weeks. All I wanted was to be by myself."

"You seem to be all right now."

Laura poured a little red wine into her glass.

"I expected...well, I wasn't sure what to expect. It was awful. I expected you to lose it, but you didn't."

"Like Hannah," he said. "Poor kid. She really let loose. I almost did, too. When I pushed that rider down to the ground, I was so pissed—the *arrogance*—but I refused to let myself feel the way I had when Libby died. I had to keep my head."

"You deserve some credit. It happened so fast, but keeping your cool was the right thing to do."

He stood.

"I'm ashamed to admit this, but what finally calmed me was the thought that it was a blessing."

John placed his long-stemmed glass into the sink.

"My best man died of cancer. It was terrible. My dad would have lingered, too, but Jamella, she handled it no problem. Jamella called for help right away. She hates noise, right? And it was *loud*, but she stayed calm. Amazing."

Laura, now by the sink with John said, "I gave her two Tylenol. She's really grown so much since she found the barn and met your dad. I would've never guessed it. In fact, I didn't want her to go back, but it worked out."

She placed her hand on his forearm and added, "For all of us."

John looked into Laura's eyes, the comfort of her friendship and support made him feel love for her. He leaned forward and kissed her gently, awkwardly.

"Let's try that again," John said, and she slid closer into his arms.

30

iana, the hospital social worker asked Lucia, "How are you feeling today?"

Lucia sat in a chair by the window in the room, hands in her lap, eyes staring at the street below.

Diana was thin limbed and wore her brown hair in a ponytail. With pale hands and blue polished nails, Diana held a tablet and cellphone. She leaned closer to Lucia, her collared shirt pocket opening to reveal a few, "While You Were Out" phone message notes.

Lucia placed her arms on the chair rest.

"I'm calm now," she said.

"Do you mind?" Diana said, motioning to the bed.

Seated upon the mattress and sheet, her perforated clogs dangled above the floor. What happens when it rains? Lucia thought of the shoes.

"Calm's good," she said, smiling. "Quiet is a nice place to be."

Lucia reflexively touched the bandage covering the wound from the since removed IV drip.

"I can go home now," she said.

"That's what I'm here to assess," Diana said. "Just want to chat a bit first. You had quite a day."

Lucia nodded, annoyed she had to convince the young woman of her mental health, but did speak to Diana of what happened and how it affected her. The young woman listened intently and asked Lucia clarifying questions that gave her confidence to speak openly. When finished, Lucia felt as if she had a better understanding of the previous day, as the swirl of sound and action unraveled itself into a timeline Lucia could process.

"He was a good man," Lucia said, her voice cracking.

After a moment, the social worker said, "He was. And he obviously felt the same about you. No? Why are you shaking your head?"

"Do you know all the pain I gave him?" Lucia said, turning her eyes to the window and the parking lot below.

"In fact, I do. You've got some tragic history for sure, but how he felt about you is his business. You must've won his heart."

Lucia looked into Diana's bright eyes, then laughed.

"It wasn't me. It was a young girl. She brought us together."

"Well, I'd like to meet her. She must be something."

Lucia nodded, "She is."

Later, she was given prescriptions for sleep and anxiety. Midafternoon, Jesus arrived to bring her home.

On the drive he asked, "So what now, Little Sister? Are you ready to come work with me? Need you to price jobs."

"In a day or two," Lucia said, thinking of the social worker and the idea that she had no control over how others felt.

Andres had texted four times and despite their being apart, she was touched by his concern. He was an "only if"—only if he wasn't married—and she smiled.

"Ah," Jesus said teasingly. "Happy thoughts about painting with me?"

"*Ajá.* I don't mind it."

She arranged for Andres to visit that night.

He came late, causing her to walk to the street-side window every few minutes until he arrived. What she needed for the moment was a companion, someone who would offer comfort and arms to hold her. Andres was tired, having finished painting a kitchen for an elderly widow, then taking a quick shower before their visit.

"Lots of cut-in work," he said, of the brushwork needed around the wall cabinets and appliances.

They sat on the aluminum lawn chairs on the back porch, the yard below quiet, the sky clear and filled with stars. He listened to Lucia, who struggled to keep her composure.

When she stopped, he took her hand and said, "He's with his wife now. He wanted you to live your life. Give you a chance for happiness."

Lucia sighed.

"I can't cry anymore. I'll never deserve what he did for me."

Andres held her hand and listened to her breathe, the quiet creating a pause to reflect.

"Maybe just accept his gift? Make the best of it."

She leaned against his shoulder.

"Will you stay? Tonight, at least," but she didn't wait for an answer because she knew he would.

Instead, Lucia looked up into the heavens, and felt a depth of unconditional love she had not felt since she was a child. It was not love based on passion or longing but the kind that gives one a sense of warmth, hope, and the confidence that the next day will be better than the last.

Mister Skip, thank you.

She soon dozed, and Andres gently woke her. When he offered to sleep on the couch, she let him. Lucia and Andres spread a sheet over the cushions.

"I'll be up at five-thirty," he said. "Do you want me to wake you?"

Lucia nodded.

"We'll have breakfast."

She kissed his cheek good night.

Later, in bed, she curled into a ball, blankets to her chin, and let the cuddled warmth remind her of those who had always believed in her worth when she did not. Lucia's dreams were of the dirt bikes, the noise, the rock, and Skip but instead of panic, she held the old man close until his soul floated away with the clouds.

John woke early to find Jamella standing by the couch, waiting for him.

"Oh. How long have you been up?"

"It's time to go to the barn. Come on."

John was halfway up the hill following Jamella when he paused, his heart popping.

"Meet me in the barn," she said, and he barely acknowledged her.

So much for jogging, he thought, as the girl scooted to the top.

"Don't wait for me," he said sarcastically, as she disappeared.

"Nice to be young, huh?" Laura said, standing on the back porch. "I wanted to see if you could keep up."

"No chance," he said.

Laura wore a blue bathrobe, flip-flops, no makeup, and a pink towel around her wet hair.

John liked how Laura was Laura. No pretense, no rushing to wear makeup or make herself presentable. He plodded on, pausing to regain his wind at the top. Entering the barn, he saw the girl adding fresh water to Cal's trough. Ace followed her, tail wagging.

His mind flashed to Libby, then to what was now gone—his boyhood home—and the emptiness of the space once filled with two horses, a garden, friends, mother and father. He allowed himself a moment to be empty, sad, alone. Where would he be now without Jamella and Laura? Another odd twist of fate had brought this mixed-race child and her mom into his life. John leaned against the barn door, the strength and grace of gratitude lifting his spirit.

"Hey, kid. Need a hand?"

John led Ace outside, watching as the dog sniffed among the stones and clumps of earth. The yellow caution tape placed by the police fluttered gently. The sun shone on the front of the barn and the air was warm and dry.

"Going to be a beautiful day."

Jamella handed a dog leash to John.

"You'll need this."

"I'm going to leave Ace here during the week. I'll check on him at noon. And what about you? Are you good to go to school tomorrow?"

Jamella nodded.

"Mister Skip told me to be ready. To keep going, in case something happened."

"Hmm. He said the same thing to me more than once. You seem to be doing that just fine."

"I'm doing it for him. Come on, Ace," she called, motioning for the dog to follow her to the house. "How long does this stupid caution tape have to stay up?"

"Guess I'll find out today," John said.

At the back porch he offered, "I know it's what dad wanted, but it's hard to get over something sad. It took me years."

He waited for the girl to respond, but she instead unlocked the door and went into the kitchen. She refreshed Ace's water and food bowls.

Patting the dog, she said, "I know what's sad and unfair like you do, but I never really had a place to live in like this."

John hung the leash on the coat rack by the door.

Jamella never looked at him as she spoke, with an almost dreamlike lilt to her voice.

"You're right," he said, "I was lucky. But I plan on being sad for a while."

"For me, it's like there's always been this weird music playing in my head telling me nothing good ever lasts."

They waited for Ace to finish his dog chow before leaving.

John said, "Things are going to be better for us, I hope!"

With a tease in her voice she said, "Glad you're so sure. But seriously, Cal and Ace are going to be lonely."

"We'll figure something out," he said, as Ace hopped onto Skip's recliner.

They stepped outside.

As they walked John said, "You've learned to handle things well. I'm impressed."

"I was an 'only' for a long time, so..."

John thought he heard her say, lonely, but before he could be sure, she was already heading down the hill.

In the afternoon, Laura walked with John and Jamella, as the girl led the horse down a trail to the brook with Ace sneaking off to follow a scent, then returning.

"This is what we loved the best," John said, "taking the horses out on the trails."

They let Jamella walk ahead while they strolled, Laura's arm within John's.

"Dad was quiet. Mom did most of the talking. I didn't think much of it, but now I realize his time in the service stuck with him. The trails, the barn, and the animals, it was all a way to relax."

"Drawing, too," Jamella said from ten paces ahead. "He liked making straight lines."

"He did," John said, smiling. "And square corners, leveled wall pictures, you name it. It had to be just right."

Laura said, "That's a dad thing, because mine was the same way. 'No-eyeballing it,' he'd say."

"That was a part of growing up in the fifties and the whole being a man-thing," John said. "Like knowing how to change the oil or grilling with charcoal."

"Thank god gas grills came out," Laura said. "Had too many burnt-to-a-crisp hamburgers."

They laughed, following the trail as it dipped toward the brook. The scent of early blooming purple lilacs growing near an open field, floated in the air.

"Wow, those flowers smell great!" Jamella said.

"They do," John said. "They were my mom's favorite. I never thought much about my mom and dad back then, and their lives. I can only wonder what Dad carried around with him after the war. And then when mom and Libby went, I fell apart, but he hung on. Way more tough-minded, I guess."

Laura said, "Takes a lot of energy to hold that in. The sad part is no one knows. It's a silent burden. I know for sure I'd have struggled."

They gave Jamella permission to walk ahead, while they stood near the open field.

After the girl had walked away, John said, "I let it out and it wasn't pretty."

"I can't imagine how awful that was. I would've never asked Gloria..."

John wrapped her into his arms.

"Forget that, it worked out well. Dad really liked her."

"Who would've guessed?" Laura said, her eyes bright.

She kissed John lightly on the lips. "So now what?"

He laughed. "Now? We go find a girl with a horse."

He squeezed her to his chest.

"After Wednesday, we can sit and decide our futures. How's that?"

They strolled to the brook where they found Ace, Cal and Jamella, on hands and knees, all sipping the water flowing between the rounded, smooth stones.

"Ugh!" Laura said. "Jamella, that's not good for you."

The girl sat back on her legs.

"It's okay. Mister Skip and I drank some every time. Are we going to cross here?"

Laura noted the cool, late afternoon shadows moving to fill the spaces between the trees.

"No," she said, "let's head back."

31

"So, you're still planning on Canada?" Lucia probed, while seated at the kitchen table on Monday morning. She was in her apartment eating breakfast with Andres who, again, had slept on the couch.

He nodded, while chewing his buttered toast.

"Paperwork is in. We'll see. You look better this morning."

"I had good dreams," she said, between sips of coffee.

"I hope that's good for both of us," he said, cleaning his dish by the sink. "Text if you need anything."

"Don't move away without letting me know first. You've been good for me."

They hugged briefly at the door before he left. It was six o'clock, and the sun was up, light filling the apartment. She thought of Jamella, who would head soon to the barn. Had it been even three full weeks that she'd taken care of Skip? Yet, she felt they were like family. She would miss sitting on the back porch with the old man in the morning and the big pot of coffee they shared, refilling his cup when it had grown cold. Carefully wiping his mouth, then later making lunch, laughing at the things he said, even when some of them never made sense. She thought of her mother and father and how she would've liked to have spent more time with them.

Lucia was struck by how time passed quickly, unlike her time in prison. She was grateful for Skip, his willingness to forgive, and his foresight. Maybe Skip's age and life experiences had factored into his decisions. She did not believe his wife had guided him from the beyond, but smiled at the thought, happy wife, happy life. But the power of forgiveness—and kindness—was not lost on her, and it roused her from her low moments. Lucia's thoughts then went to the frizzy-haired, brown-skinned girl with the splash of freckles under her eyes. She had not considered how the girl or her mother might be feeling.

Her cellphone rang.

"I was just thinking of you," Lucia said.

Laura called to invite her to brunch with Jamella and Hannah.

"We, Hannah's mom and I, thought it would be good for us to not take the girls to school today. It's better for all of us. Give me your address and we'll pick you up."

Lucia sat in the back of Laura's SUV with Jamella and Hannah, who said kids texted her with, "Too many questions," she said. "Kids can be weird."

Laura resisted the urge to add that adults can be, too.

Instead, she said, "We thought a day to just go easy would be good."

At a restaurant known for its breakfast burritos, Lucia ordered an egg-white omelet.

"I've never had one without the yoke," she said, causing an awkward pause. "Don't serve them in prison," she continued, acknowledging the obvious. "Food was blah. Like school lunch, right?"

"I hate the cafeteria," Jamella said. "All the noise and yucky smells."

Hannah laughed, and Kathy's eyes brightened.

"Can we get our hair done today?" Jamella asked.

Lucia knew of the salon, so after breakfast they went together and had their hair and nails done. Discussing what hairstyles and nail colors to choose was a pleasant distraction. No one spoke of the rider, Tyler Digby's arrest for trespassing and involuntary manslaughter, or of the news that followed it. Instead, they focused on what fit them best.

Jamella decided on a ponytail that pulled her frizzy hair back from her face, while Hannah kept hers shoulder length, but parted in the middle.

"Don't we look good?" Kathy said, after they had left.

Like brand new, Lucia thought.

Jamella wanted to visit Lucia's apartment, so they drove to her home.

After a short tour, Jamella said, "It's kind of plain, but the porch is high. Do you ever see anything cool?"

"Like?" Lucia asked.

"Long Eared Owls, maybe?" Laura said, teasingly. "You know, that's how this all started. Jamella chased an owl into Skip's barn. That's how we all became friends."

"That's nice," Kathy said, her words leaving them to their thoughts.

After they'd gone, Lucia stepped out onto the back porch. Looking at the horizon, she took note of the office buildings, cars, and those walking along busy streets. It was time to build a life.

32

John sat with Ed Wilson at the police station after signing the witness statement. It was early Monday evening, and he thought of Ace alone at the house.

"So," John said, "this is all you need from me, right?"

Wilson nodded.

"We have the video, statements, and the other rider is cooperating. Once we brought her in, she told us he planned to drive through the yard as a "screw-you" to your dad. Once she realized what happened, she gave a detailed statement. Cut and dried, just like that last time."

Wilson paused. He extended a hand to John.

"Sorry, didn't mean to bring that up. When's the wake?"

They shook hands.

"No wake, just a mass on Wednesday at ten. He wanted to be cremated, so..."

"Veterans Cemetery?"

"No, at Saint Maria's with my mom. You don't need any other statements, do you?"

"Not at this time. If something changes, I'll let you know. I'm sure the kid, Digby, will have a good lawyer. His uncle has money, but if he's smart, he'll plead. A trial won't help."

John arrived home to find Ace waiting for him. He patted the dog's head. Once outside, Ace wandered to a spot behind the rhododendron bushes. When he returned, they walked to the barn.

Inside, Cal was chewing the last of the hay that Jamella had left for him earlier. The barn was neater than when he had been responsible for it as a young man.

"You've never had it so good," he said to the horse.

Sitting on his father's curved bale of hay, he said, "I had it good, too," and he thought of Skip.

When John was a boy, his taller-than-most-dads—a war veteran who could run a farm, ride a horse, throw a baseball, and handle every problem that came his way—was larger than life. The boy hurried home from school to await Skip's arrival and listen to the news of the day or to help with any chore.

On Saturdays, he'd ride the trails, at first with his dad in front, and later, he would lead, head held high as they went to the brook that beavers had turned into a small pond. Man and boy rode quietly, John content to be drawn within his father's physical orbit and lulled by the soft clumping of hooves and thrilling of birds. They spoke of what was practical, school grades, weather, a broken fence, or sports teams—manly things—that made the boy feel grownup. But then, of course, he became a teenager, and his father's mythical stature became a nuisance, an obstacle, a reason to be mad at the world.

He sighed.

The chance to reconnect with Skip after the deaths of Eloise and Libby had disintegrated, appropriately, like ash.

The sound of tires riding on gravel roused him.

Officer Wilson, on his way home, stopped to tell John that Digby was, "in the wind." He rubbed at the circles under his eyes. "Be alert. I'd guess he's long gone, but can't be too careful. Can you let the neighbor know?" he said, motioning with his thumb toward Laura's.

John nodded.

"Unreal. So much for hoping the kid would plead."

Wilson, with his hands on his hips said, "It's just a matter of time. He's a spoiled kid with a rich uncle who gave him bad advice. He's a militia wannabe. Probably armed. I'll keep you updated. Oh, and you might hear from the press. We have to put out a notice, so that'll alert them."

"You're just full of good news," John said, and Wilson shrugged.

"We'll get him. Obviously not the brightest bulb."

As Wilson drove away, John called Laura.

"That's worrisome," she said.

Her mind spun to adding more security cameras and lights, GPS location tags for Jamella, and letting the school district know of the risk.

"How much of a threat is he?"

"According to Wilson, they'll get him soon. I hoped he'd plead and go to jail so we could get past this. Now, we've got this to deal with... Hold on, I've got another call."

Laura walked to each window and looked out into the dark yard.

When John disconnected, he said, "If there's a call from the local news, tell them no comment. That's what I just did."

"Oh, no, that's the least of my worries," she said, her voice distant.

John heard the snaps of window latches, as Laura moved through the house.

"I'll bring Ace over. He's a good watch dog."

Jamella and Laura were at the back door when John arrived with Ace, his tail wagging, ears perked.

"Come on," the girl said, leading the dog to her bedroom.

Laura said softly, "She thinks you have to work tonight. I'll tell her in the morning. Kathy and I are going to bring the girls to school. We want to be sure there's a safety plan.

And Gloria's aware. I'm meeting with her brother tomorrow about more security cameras and motion lights. Do you want in on that?"

John nodded, thinking about how Cal was alone.

"Wow, you've done all that in ten minutes?"

"No time to waste time, right? I told them I'd call again after I spoke to you."

John reached out and held her hands.

"Right. I'll call if I learn anything new."

He kissed her lips lightly.

Before heading outside he said, "Can you make sure I can see the barn and the corral with the cameras? And I'll meet Jamella again in the morning when she comes to feed Cal."

Laura teased, "Be careful going back up that hill."

And he was.

He went slowly, moving from one tree branch to another, careful not to slide off the wide, round rocks wet with the night's dew. John paused at the top to catch his breath. He looked back at Laura's and saw Jamella wave to him from the bathroom before she turned out the light. From this angle, the house was vulnerable, and he considered all the ways someone with bad intent could harm them. Feeling a bit edgy, he decided to check on Cal.

He stepped inside, deciding against turning on the lights. The solitary horse stood in its corral, a black shadow with only its eyes barely visible. A mouse scurried over the toes of his left shoe. In the darkness, the barn was cavernous.

"Sorry, Cal," he said with guilt. "This isn't right. I'm going to get you a companion."

Cal's isolation made John think of Gloria, prison, and of all the time he and Skip had spent apart and alone. The tragic loss of his mother and daughter created an invisible cell of grief. John wondered if he would have handled death better if he, too, had witnessed a man step in front of a moving freight train or the deaths of soldiers under his command. But what made him think Skip had a better handle on living and dying when we are all susceptible to unimaginable loss? No, John had it all wrong. Grief was all around us, he knew, inflicted by happenstance or by one upon the other, and no one was immune. John had grieved enough. It was time to prevent as much of it as he could for others, the key of which lied in the simple acts of empathy and kindness.

Later, he scoured the internet for old horses. Plenty of them needed a home, so he arranged that night for two, the maximum corral space available, to be delivered on the upcoming Saturday and Sunday morning.

John turned the laptop computer off, closed his eyes, and listened to the subtle sounds of the empty home: the buzz of a running refrigerator, the metallic ticking of the oven clock, and the occasional roar of a heavy-duty truck on the highway. A sadness for what was lost came over him, but rather than letting the hurt take him to a darker place, he accepted it as a part of who he was and how he would live.

John went to bed feeling that his parents would approve of adding two horses. He smiled as he thought of Jamella and having to clean after three horses. *Time for her to earn an allowance!*

33

At five a.m., John stood behind the barn with a flashlight, waiting for Jamella. He shivered, and looked into the trees to the right, but nothing stirred.

Laura's backdoor opened and Jamella popped out onto the porch.

John waved to Laura, who stood wearing her go-to blue bathrobe, and with her hair uncombed. He liked how she was comfortable without makeup. It gave him a sense of trust and connection.

"Good morning," John said to the girl standing before him.

She wore rubber boots and work gloves over a pair of jeans and a long-sleeved shirt.

"Why are you here?" she asked, looking at him with one eye squinted.

"I have a surprise for you."

"Oh, like mom taking me to school today? She said I could ask you why. Mom doesn't like talking so early."

Inside the barn John said, "Guess there's two surprises then. Let's get the bad one out of the way. Ready?"

Jamella was filling Cal's water trough, so John wasn't sure she'd heard. She turned the water spigot off.

"Ready," she said, arms by her side.

"The guy on the bike ran away and the police are looking for him. That's why you're getting a ride to school today. The school needs to know of a potential thr—uh, person to look out for."

Jamella pressed her lips together and nodded.

"Are you okay with that?" John asked.

"I don't like the bus so, yeah, a ride's cool."

John smiled.

"That's good, but, no, I meant with this biker guy being loose. We have to be on the alert."

"Okay, but I don't know what he looks like, except for the weird tattoo. He had the letters 'P' and 'B' on his hand inside a circle, so that's easy."

"He does? You saw that? Everything happened so fast. You're pretty sharp."

He walked with her out of the barn as she led Cal to the field.

"It's how my brain works. Things just pop into it, good and bad."

The sunrise was leaking in through the trees, and the morning dew hung in the air. She stood in the gray, damp mist, her eyes sharp.

"I've had to keep an eye on my stuff since forever. I'm good at it."

Before turning toward home, she asked, "What's the good news?"

"Right, almost forgot. I arranged for two old horses to come live here with Cal. One on Saturday and one on Sunday, both lady horses. Thought Cal could use some company, but I can't handle them alone. Interested in making five bucks a week?"

Jamella leaned forward, her eyes squinted.

"Wait, what? You bought more horses? Cal's not going to be an only? How did you find them?"

"I didn't buy them. The owners couldn't care for them. I want to pay you to help, too."

"Sure!" she said. "That'll be awesome! We'll have to make room for them."

"We'll start tonight. We need two more stalls cleaned out."

Later, on the ride with Laura to school, she couldn't stop thinking about the new horses and spoke non-stop about preparing the barn for their arrival.

Laura would thank John later for taking Jamella's mind off Digby, who Laura felt was a wildcard. Would he be far away, a fugitive, or close by looking for revenge? Although her clients would keep her busy, she found her mind wandering when a hooded young man walked by her office window, or when a group of men stepped out of a van at the convenience store. Everyone became a suspect. Laura developed a tension headache, and left at noon. She was happy to be home, the smell of beef stew slowly cooking in a crockpot soothed her.

Upon returning from school, Jamella changed clothes and met John in the barn. When asked about her day she explained how everyone had been nice to her.

"Almost too nice," she said, not mentioning that the bus bullies, Mike and Kevin, stared at her the whole ride home.

Jamella was used to being stared at, but now she kept a metal pen handy in case someone tried to jump her. The girl had fought with both girls and boys and learned fists were painful and powerful. It was also a means to an end, and she would defend herself and her possessions, no matter the result, but preferred to mind her own business.

When calm, she could feel the vibrations of light and color that inspired her drawings, so she avoided conflict.

"That sounds better than my day," John said, wiping the inside of a second galvanized water bucket. "Two news crews came to the house, but I asked them to respect our privacy, and they eventually left."

"What's it like to lose your dad?" she asked, head turned from John.

He paused, watching as she pulled a coil of rope from under a pile of new fence posts. He noticed for the first time that her hips were wider, and she had gained a bit of weight.

"Do you want the short answer or the long one?"

"Short."

"I feel sad about it. I could've been a better son."

"How?"

John pulled his jeans up at the hip.

"Now that's the long answer."

Jamella's lack of response encouraged John to add, "I let the car accident create a space between us. It's as if our lives ended when my mom and Libby died."

"But he was the dad. He should've tried, too."

John leaned on the handle of the push broom.

Jamella was taller, her face fuller. She was no longer a child, but a young adult who should know what was true.

He said, "Maybe, sure, but I felt guilty about the accident. I should've driven Libby to school that day. I was ashamed, even though he didn't think it was my fault."

The girl clapped the dust from her hands.

"Do you hate Gloria?"

"Yes and no. She reminds me of what happened, but she took good care of my dad, who liked her. Here, hold this gate open so I can sweep out the old hay."

As he and Jamella worked together, they heard, "Oh, my!"

Laura stood outside by the door waving away a cloud of dust.

Jamella sneezed, then John did, and they laughed.

"Time for dinner, but you're not coming in with that filth on you."

John started the air compressor, covered with cobwebs, sitting by an electrical box. He buzzed Jamella with it, knocking the dust from her clothes. When he stuck the nozzle under the back of her shirt, she jumped.

"Okay," John said, "my turn."

Jamella, when finished with the air hose, goosed John's back as well.

"We're even," he said with a smile.

On the walk back, and with Jamella out of earshot, John said, "I know she's close to Gloria. I wouldn't get in the way of that, but I would rather not have to deal with her much. Is that okay?"

"Of course. Sounds like you're thinking big picture."

Laura stopped. With hands on hips and a tilt of her chin she said, "Like maybe going steady with me?"

"Yup, but *slow* and steady. I want to make sure this business with the biker is done with, first."

After dinner, Jamella read from a sheet of lined paper, written in perfect cursive. She asked if she could read what she'd written at church.

"Oh?" Laura said, surprised that Jamella wouldn't be too shy.

"Sure. Let's hear it," John said.

Jamella cleared her throat.

"Mister Frank, 'Skip,' Lowell was my first grown-up best friend. I had to prove I was responsible enough to take care of his horse, Cal, and his dog, Ace, or they would suffer from neglect. He told me this because he knew they would need me when he died. So, I figured out how to keep my mind focused on what was important. You don't know me, but noise and light distract me, and Mister Skip wanted me to learn how to deal with it. Oh yeah, he used blackmail, but it worked, and I love him for that. He was like a grandfather to me, and I'll never forget him."

After a moment, Laura spoke.

"That was so nice! I'd wondered how you'd gotten your grades to improve."

Jamella, cheeks flushed with pride said, "Hannah helped me, too."

"Good friend to have," John said. "Wow. Dad would love that. You'll be great tomorrow."

"You won't be nervous?" Laura asked.

Jamella shook her head. But later, in bed, she dreamt of men and women wearing large, black shiny helmets seated in the pews. When she'd finished speaking, they rose as one and came for her. She panicked and called for help, but neither Laura, John, nor Hannah understood what was wrong. Just as the silent, oppressive mob closed around her, she woke, her throat dry, chest heaving.

Sitting up, she woke Ace sleeping at the foot of her bed. The dog opened one eye.

"Sorry. Just a bad dream."

Jamella grabbed the worn, stuffed butterfly and tucked it under her pillow before dozing off.

34

John woke on the morning of the funeral to the first light of the day shining off an oval, football-sized mirror. When he was a young man, he would drape a towel or tee shirt over it so he could sleep later. He smiled. The mirror was his last stop before going out with friends or a date.

"Old reliable," he said of the mirror as he slid his legs into a pair of pants.

He was to meet Jamella at six a.m. this day.

"Let's sleep in tomorrow," he had said to her.

His thoughts then turned to what he would say about his father during the church service, but the words wouldn't come.

He looked into the mirror and saw gray hair at his temples, an extra chin where there had not been one, and wrinkles by his eyes. The inevitability of growing old stared back.

"Geez, I'm getting old."

No words came to mind as he trudged down the stairs. His eye landed on Skip's faded and well-worn green recliner. John paused. The anchors of his life, Skip and Eloise, were gone and he was momentarily disoriented. What had held John's boyhood was now just any other old home. The tide of life had come and gone, washing away their footprints. With his hand on the chair's headrest, he decided he would say what all sons say about their fathers; beyond that, there wasn't much more to add. He had lost his father years ago.

He drove Laura and Jamella to the church. They said little, except for John who noted that Jamella gave Cal a long hug earlier in the morning. The horse and dog miss Mister Skip, she said, and Laura added that they did, too.

They were dressed in black, Jamella wearing a skirt and matching top. Laura also wore a gray, light cotton sweater over her bare arms, while John had on a suit with wrinkled pants. John had dropped his faith years ago. It was part of what was lost over time. Laura attended only on special occasions, as the Catholic Church's uncompromising edicts frustrated her. Jamella admired the stained glass windows and faded ceiling art.

They sat in the first pew, Skip's urn and military portrait on a table in front of the altar and waited for the service to begin. Jamella sat between John and Laura, clutching the paper upon which her eulogy was written. John asked if she was all set to read it before the others and she nodded.

"Are you?" she asked.

"Not really," John said with a shrug, and the girl's eyes widened.

Although she knew of the funeral arrangements, Gloria worked instead with her brother and Andres to install security. They arrived early at Laura's and went about like ghosts so as not to disturb their employer. While discussing the phone application for the video equipment, Gloria quietly mentioned to Laura that she would not attend the mass and Laura understood.

It took two hours to set up the equipment at Laura's but took longer at John's. The weathered and faded caution tape tied to wooden stakes surprised Gloria. Like Jamella had, she felt anger at the fluttering reminder of Skip's death. *So unfair!* But guilt overcame her. She had inflicted pain upon the poor man and his family and now that same pain produced a hurt she had never experienced, even after her loved ones had died.

Falling to her knees, she said, "I'm sorry, Mister Skip. I will be a better person."

With her eyes closed, the long lingering blackness from within her soul covered her with a funereal shroud. She felt as if life had left her behind. The warmth of Jesus' arm around her shoulders caused her to sigh.

"Why is it only the bad for me?"

Jesus held his sister for a minute.

"Shh," he said. "Be still. Listen for his voice."

Jesus referred to God, but she listened for Skip's, and eventually the thought of the old man chiding her for loafing on the job roused her. Jesus helped her to stand on wobbly legs.

"All set?" he asked.

When she nodded, he walked with her to the barn. Inside, he noted the changes.

"Looks like your little friend has been hard at work," Jesus said, while Gloria wondered what Jamella, or John, had planned for the new space.

"She's a worker," Jesus said, with a respectful nod of his head.

Jamella was unaware of Jesus' comments as she stood at the church lectern, looking at the parishioners before her. She did notice one black man seated in the back, wondered why he was there, cleared her throat and then began. As she spoke, heads nodded and smiled, and she was pleased. Their silent approval of her eulogy made Jamella feel closer to Skip, and sense that she belonged. Her words, echoing within the mostly empty space, brought Skip's loss home. As she walked, tears formed on her cheeks.

John took her place at the lectern. He took a deep breath and then thanked those who came. He, too, noticed the black face behind those seated closer to the front. The man was thin with short, curly white hair and a scruffy white beard. He sat with his back straight and eyes focused. Military, John thought. He began.

"My Dad was a quiet man who believed in doing one's best. He was a creature of habit, but a great father and husband. He also never missed a chance to needle me when it was deserved."

At this, some of the parishioners smiled so John added, "Some of you seem to know what I mean."

He then continued.

"Over the past few weeks, especially, I have come to realize that I was a lucky boy. My mom, Eloise, and dad, kept me in line. I never went without anything, and they encouraged me to do my best. Dad was not just a hero who served in Vietnam, but my hero, too. He gave me great advice when we lost my daughter, Libby, and his wife, my mom, Eloise. But I couldn't handle it.

In that sense, I let him down. He told me to put one foot in front of the other, but I crashed and burned and it created a distance between us. I was selfish with my grief, held it too close, and lost my wife, home, and a few jobs. I didn't understand that what he really wanted for me was not to just grind along but be available to others.

Life can be hard and cruel, and we deal with it in our own ways, but I should've taken a moment to think and listen. But I didn't. The perceptive young woman who you met a minute ago asked me why I wasn't angry with my dad for not reaching out to me. Good question. In his way, he did reach out, but he wasn't one to push. He gave me space, but I took too much of it, and left the burden on him. Would it have been so hard to meet him halfway?

"So, Dad," John swallowed, clearing his throat. "I'm sorry. You were and will forever be a better man. I know, too, that you'll always be with me, probably because you're sure that I'll mess something up!

"Seriously, though, I'm ready now to put one foot in front of the other and try to be the man you hoped I would become and to be available to others, to do some good. Thank you, Dad."

John looked at the churchgoers, and noticed the smile on the black man's face. He would later learn the man's name, Benny, and that he served under Skip in Vietnam.

Of John's eulogy, Benny, with his raspy voice said, "That was the man I knew, too. Always tried to do the right thing, but sometimes the job was too big."

"Did you keep in touch?"

"I'd see him occasionally at the V.F.W. post, but not for quite a while now. I wanted to pay my respects."

He took a step away but stopped.

He asked, "Oh, did I hear right? He saved a woman's life?"

John nodded.

"Stood in front of her, blocked some flying stones."

"Hmm. Once a soldier..."

"Always a soldier," John finished.

Benny put a warm hand on John's shoulder.

"He'd be proud of you."

"That means a lot. Thank you. When's a good night to stop into the hall? It would be great to have a beer or two."

Benny smiled.

"Hump day, eighteen hundred hours."

He then bent to speak to Jamella, his black suit a size too big.

"That was definitely Lieutenant Lowell. Blackmail, ha! But you had to work hard to be his friend. He wasn't touchy-feely, so good. You *earned* his friendship."

"That was kind of him," Laura said to John after the man had left. "He waited until he was the last in line to wish us well. Not that it was too long."

"Not like the last time," John said, wistfully. "It took two exhausting sessions. People were lined up outside. I mean, it's well meaning, but it's tough. Today was just right. And I may meet Benny for a beer. He could fill me in on my dad's time in Vietnam."

"No relatives to ask?"

"An older brother, Sam, but he died. Stroke. He lived on the west coast."

"So, you're an only," Laura said, bringing a smile to his face.

"I'm hoping not," he said, reaching for her hand as they walked to the parking lot. "You didn't mind that I introduced you as my girlfriend, did you?"

"Keep the good behavior up and we'll see," she said with a playful tug of his hand.

"Are you going to get married in this church?" Jamella asked.

"Gee, do people still do that?" John teased.

"Yes," Jamella said emphatically.

"You're getting a little ahead of yourself," he said, putting an arm around the girl's shoulder.

"Yeah. So, I don't know what that means."

Laura added, "It's the same as counting your chickens before they hatch."

Jamella, arms folded across her chest said, "Now, how can you count them before they hatch? They're still eggs, not chickens."

Looking at each other, John and Laura laughed.

"You two think you're so smart, but you're just weirdos. You know that, right?"

Jesus had set up the cameras before John, Laura, and Jamella returned home in the early afternoon. He left a bill in her mailbox.

"Aww," Jamella said. "I thought Gloria would still be here."

Laura downloaded the surveillance app to John's phone and then showed him how it worked.

"Ticks me off that we have to do this," he said, holding the cell phone. "I guess rules don't apply to some people."

After dinner, John and Jamella walked up the back hill to the barn. At the crest, Jamella paused.

"It's that jerky guy," she said, of the owner of the black Cadillac, parked in John's driveway.

"He was the one who offered my dad some money, right?" John said, and Jamella nodded.

They watched as the man pushed on the back door, peeking through the door's half window light. He stepped away from the porch, hands on hips, an ample belly hanging over his suit belt.

"Can we help you," John called as they approached.

The man turned. He flattened his windblown, gray-streaked brown hair.

Pulling up his pants he said, "I'm looking for the owner. I'm Al Digby."

John crossed his arms.

"He's not here. But you knew that didn't you?"

The man shrugged, his puffy eyes thinly visible. He flattened his red tie.

"Can we talk? Privately?"

John looked at Jamella.

"You can stay," he said.

"No. I'd rather see Cal."

After she'd left Al said, "Look, sorry about what happened. That's my knuckleheaded nephew for you. Now this wouldn't have happened if your father hadn't pressed charges, but no matter. Let's make the best of a bad situation. I'm willing to offer you seven hundred thousand for the place. What do you say?"

John felt anger rising but held it.

"What do I say?" he said, firmly. "Get lost. I'm not interested."

"You'd throw almost a million away? Look around, this place needs lots of work. Why kill yourself? Use the money to move to your dream house."

"I asked you to leave." John pointed to the Cadillac. "Now." John reached for his cellphone. "Or I make a call."

Digby, hands on hips, shook his head.

"Just like your old man, stubborn. Offered him enough money to put on a new roof, or replace the windows. Maybe a driveway. This yard's pathetic."

John stared at the man standing in the dark shadow of the porch overhang, who said, "Think it over."

"I have. It all makes sense now. Have your nephew dump trash and harass him, right? Get him fed up enough to sell. Just an old man, how hard could it be? Too bad you relied on a screw-up."

"My nephew wasn't the problem. It was that 'thing' over there," he said with a nod of his head toward Jamella. "You saying she's that important to you, her and the plain Jane she lives with, that you'd walk away from big bucks? Eight hundred, last offer."

"Nope. Don't want anything to do with you or that criminal nephew of yours."

"Don't worry. *You'll* never see him again. But he might decide to see you first. He can be stubborn. Keep that in mind," Digby said, walking to the car.

John stared at the man as he turned and drove off. Would his nephew return? No doubt, if his uncle asked.

He said, "Now I know why you kept guns by the doors, Dad."

But he wouldn't sell the property. Instead, he would take Skip's advice to subdivide the acreage by the main road. Laura could help with the logistics.

Later as they sat in John's kitchen, he discussed the idea with Laura and her thoughts on the financials. Over an empty, stained pizza box with a few bits of uneaten crust, she spoke of a real estate agent who would help.

When the doorbell rang, John flinched. He took a breath and put Digby out of his mind.

Jesus and Gloria stood on the porch, asking to speak to John.

Hat in hand, dressed in blue slate work pants and shirts with a "JM Painting" logo on the pocket, Jesus said, "My sister and I would like to express our condolences."

Gloria, eyes lowered, said, "I feel your father's loss as much as I did my own," she said, her voice cracking.

Jesus said, "He was a good man. Good to my sister."

"I put a terrible burden upon you," Gloria added. "I truly understand this now. You were both better to me than I ever deserved."

Jesus extended his palm.

"Thank you," John said.

The men shook hands.

Laura and Jamella stood in the doorway, the sense of their shared pain weighing heavily upon Laura's chest. She gulped back tears as Jesus and his sister walked to the van.

Before they disappeared into the blackness of night, John said, "Lucia is dead to me, but Gloria is welcome here."

Lucia turned.

The faces of Jamella, John, and Laura were shadowed by the porch and evening light, but his words struck like thunder.

Jesus wrapped an arm around her shoulder and smiled.

"Gracias," he said.

Lucia patted her heart lightly.

"And your family will always be here."

They waved as the van rolled down the driveway. John felt the warmth of Laura and Jamella now standing close by his side. It was at this moment that Laura decided that if he was ready to love her, she was ready in return. They *would* be a family.

Jamella, though, was unsure of what she had heard, so she later asked Laura, who explained to her that what the girl had witnessed was real forgiveness.

"That's not something that happens every day."

"I know," Jamella said, nodding. "John did it for us...and Mister Skip."

Laura, standing by Jamella's bedroom desk said, "It feels good, huh?"

Jamella slid under the sheets of the bed.

"It does. Like when I take the big towels out of the dryer."

"Ah, right. A nice warm feeling," she said, lifting a sketch of Skip sitting on the body contoured bale of hay. "You're drawing again, great. John will like this."

She expected to see Jamella smile, but instead, the girl's eyes grew dark, and her good cheer dissipated.

"Do you think it will last?" she asked. "Do you think John will always like us?"

"Yes, I do, but there are no guarantees. We'll make the best of each day. And you've got my back, right?" she said with a smile.

Jamella shrugged, as a narrow smile crossed her lips.

"You're not so funny," Laura said.

The nightlight in the hall cast a soft shadow on Jamella, whose left hand moved in loops and lines on the bedsheet by her side.

35

Not that John was overly concerned about Tyler Digby and his uncle, but sleeping alone did have him on edge. Even the hubbub created when Beauty and Lady, the two adopted horses arrived on the weekend, could not distract John from worry. He had been so angry when speaking to the uncle he decided he would shoot the nephew if he had to, but now he was not so sure and found his thoughts wandering to his dad's service time. He had never asked his father what it had been like to kill a man or watch them die, or what it was like to have the lives of his men depend upon his decisions.

John had missed so many chances to learn from Skip and of the violence and resulting grief we sometimes inflict. He thought of Skip hunched over his mechanical drawing table, redoing sketches straight line after straight line. It had been his therapy, his way of sidestepping grief and regret. Skip had compartmentalized the war, but would never forget it. The later tragedy of Eloise and Libby wounded him to the core; his foundation burned to the ground. All Skip had then was Cal and later, Ace. His son went A.W.O.L. and missed a chance to deepen a relationship with the only man left who loved him.

In his sadness, John had pushed aside his father, severed himself from him, a slave to the whip snap of grief. Skip had known suffering, pain, and sadness beyond understanding, but John had passed on the chance to find solace in their shared pain. Together, they might have found a tiny gem of happiness.

"I was naïve," he would say later to Laura as they sat in her living room. "I thought life was fair, but my dad knew better. That was my biggest problem. I was always angry."

The next two weeks would keep him busy. Laura worked with a realtor to create one four-acre parcel, with the stipulation that John meet the potential buyer before the sale was agreed upon.

"Don't want Digby sneaking one by us," he said to Laura.

John and Jamella tended to the horses, barn, and the painting of his old bedroom from green to light blue. He kept the door to his parents' room closed after placing all their photos and mementos inside. In his mother's bureau, the drawers of which had remained untouched, he found photos of himself and Libby as toddlers. The eyes and cheeks were his. The master bedroom would be the last to be painted.

John and Laura dropped the, "Have you heard anything?" question of the day after a week, resigned to remaining vigilant.

"It bothers Jamella. I have to sit with her at night and go over how we're safe, you're safe, the horses, the barn...this is her family now, so there's more to lose. I have to admit, it makes me anxious," Laura said, as they sat watching the local television news in Laura's living room.

"It's in the back of my mind, too," John said, turning to face her.

Since the funeral, they had developed the routine of having dinner, watching television, and John taking over for Jamella in the barn on school nights.

"It's better to check on Cal in the morning anyway," Jamella told Laura. "Too much poop to shovel at night."

Laura laughed.

Two weeks later, on an early Saturday evening, Jamella and Hannah decided to hang the large poster-sized drawing of Skip sitting on the hay bale in the barn with Laura, Kathy, and Gloria, who now had her own used compact car.

"Been working for hospice care and with my brother, too," she explained. "No boyfriend yet, so I'm saving money."

They set two stepladders near the wall and worked to nail it in place, while John gave them space and tried to repair the sagging garden fence.

He heard the women and girls laughing, and he was content. But John had not realized how deeply despair had held him hostage until Officer Wilson called with news.

Tyler Digby, after a drunken bar fight near the US-Canadian border, was arrested.

"He's jammed himself up good, now," Wilson said. "Looking at lots of time."

John walked to where Cal stood with Beauty and Lady, his mind spinning.

The horse nodded its head and whinnied.

"That's right Cal, they got him," he said, his legs weak, chest tingling.

With his forehead pressed against Cal's, a well of electric, metallic-tasting bile filled his mouth. His eyes watered, he spit, then he sobbed.

The horse stood patiently as he moved to the horse's flank.

John, his arms wrapped around his waist, bent over and spit again.

He would later tell Laura, "My brain and stomach were on fire."

With the poster now hung in the barn, Hannah and Jamella walked outside to call John.

"What's he doing?" Jamella asked, skipping closer to him.

After a moment, Hannah said, "Oh! He's crying. All the hurt inside is coming out. You can't stop it. Mister John," she called. "Come see the poster instead!"

After she called again, he acknowledged her with a nod.

Thank God for a clean handkerchief, he thought, as he wiped snot and tears from his face. He walked slowly, using the opportunity to compose himself.

Laura, Gloria, and Kathy joined the girls by the barn entrance and watched as John walked head down, hands and arms wiping at his face. The puffy redness of his eyes worried Laura.

"Dust?" she asked, or wondering, too, if he might have been stung by a wasp.

"Digby was arrested," he said, his voice thick with emotion.

"Good news! Finally," Kathy said, while Laura wrapped her arms around John.

Gloria waved a quiet goodbye to Jamella, but before she could leave, John said, "Stay," and she did.

Inside the barn, Jamella explained why she drew Skip seated on the bale with a beer in his hand, not sleeping, but leaning forward.

"He'll always have his eye on us," Jamella said. "Just like when I first met him."

Gloria smiled.

"That's Mister Skip for sure."

"Perfect," John said. "That's just how he'd like to be remembered...sitting in his favorite place."

A fluttering of wings caused them to turn their attention to the roof beams.

"That's not a bat, is it?" Kathy said, crouching down, hands placed over her head.

"No," Jamella said, "it's a Long-Eared Owl!"

The bird turned his head as if on a swivel, its chest feathers moving up and down like piano keys.

"It's probably wondering what we all are doing here," Laura said.

"It's a part of our family now," Jamella said. "I wonder what it eats?"

"Okay, not feeding wild birds, thank you," Laura said. "Don't even think about it."

"All right," Jamella said, turning to wink at Hannah.

"Looks like it's all come full circle," Laura said to John.

John's smiling eyes met Laura's and he understood that today and tomorrow would be better days than those that had come before.

That night, as Jamella crawled into bed, she said to Laura.

"Do you know what Hannah said to me today?"

"No," Laura said, helping Jamella pull the bed sheet and blanket to the girl's chin.

"She said I was so lucky. You know because of Cal and the barn."

"You are," Laura said, moving to turn off the lamp on the nightstand.

"I know. Crazy huh? She's pretty and smart and cool, but she thinks *I'm* lucky...wow."

"Better get used to it," Laura said, snapping off the light.

The End.

About the Author

Dennis Kafalas

Dennis J. Kafalas has written several short stories, three novels: *Fortunate Son*, *An Obvious Life* and *Whale Pirates*, as well as an educational text, *Inspired Learners Active Minds: A Guide for the English Classroom.* He is a retired public school teacher and administrator, who lives with his wife, Barbara, in Glendale, RI. Please leave comments at denniskafalas.com.